RANGER COURAGE

TEXAS RANGER HEROES

LYNN SHANNON

CT
Creative Thoughts

RANGER COURAGE

This novel is dedicated to my sister, Katherine. You're amazing and the very best sister anyone could ask for. I love you.

Do not let your hearts be troubled and do not be afraid.

John 14:27

ONE

Thunder rumbled, deep enough to rattle the windows on the patrol car, and the first sprinkles of rain scattered in the wind. Avery Madison calculated she had five minutes to make it home before the storm broke. As luck would have it, one of the perks of being Harrison University's Chief of Police was a house on the outskirts of campus. Her commute was only four minutes. She longed for fuzzy pajamas and a heaping bowl of ice cream.

The radio crackled and the night dispatch

operator called for her. Avery groaned and picked up the receiver. "It's a go for Madison."

"Chief, we've gotten a request for a safety escort from the Fairman Building to the faculty parking lot. The other unit is still handling the fist fight at the fraternity house."

"10-4. I'll handle the escort," Avery said. Safety escorts were provided as a security measure on campus. Faculty or students could request a police officer to accompany them anywhere on university grounds. Avery swung her patrol car into a parking lot and pulled a U-turn. The ice cream and fuzzy pajamas would have to wait. "What's the name?"

"It's Professor Jenkins, Chief. She'll be waiting in the north entrance."

Lightning streaked across the sky and the raindrops quickened as Avery pulled into the faculty parking lot closest to the Fairman Building. There were a handful of other cars. It was more than she expected on a Friday evening, but maybe some of the professors were preparing for the last stretch of classes before spring break.

Wind carried the scent of damp grass and rain as Avery hurried across the quad to the Fairman Building. Through the glass doors, the lobby glowed with bright fluorescents. No one was standing there.

Strange. Professor Jenkins always called for an escort when she worked late, and she'd never left an officer waiting before. Avery opened the locked door with her master key. Resting on a couch in the lobby were a worn briefcase and an umbrella.

A muffled thump came from somewhere down the hall.

"Professor Jenkins?" Avery's voice echoed through the otherwise quiet building, and silence followed. A chill skirted down her spine. Her hand automatically went to her weapon, although she left it in the holster. "Professor Jenkins? It's Chief Madison."

Avery held her breath. From somewhere around the corner, there was a faint noise. Was someone...crying? A bolt of lightning streaked across the sky followed by the boom of a transformer exploding. The lights in the building went out. A wailing scream followed, sending Avery's heart into overdrive.

She pulled her weapon. The university's emergency generator kicked on. The lights overhead were dim, but sufficient enough to see. Avery moved in the direction of the scream. She forced her breathing to slow, counteracting the adrenaline racing through her veins. Her rubber-soled boots were silent against the floor.

She rounded the corner. A woman was crouched at the end of the corridor, near the stairwell. Avery immediately recognized her. Professor Jenkins's shoulders shook with the force of silent sobs. She was barefoot. A shoe, the heel broken, lay discarded in the hall.

Avery's gut clenched. "Professor Jenkins?"

The woman glanced up. She flung her hands out, backing away in a panic. "No, please no. Don't."

"Professor Jenkins, it's Chief Madison with HUPD." Avery glanced behind her and lowered the weapon, stepping farther into the light. "Ma'am, I'm the police."

The professor froze and blinked. Recognition flashed across her face. "Chief..."

"What happened?" Avery scanned the other woman. Her clothes were disheveled, although they were intact and she wasn't bleeding. Another high heel shoe rested on the stairs. Had she fallen?

"I r-r-ran." Professor Jenkins used the wall to support herself as she rose to a standing position. She swallowed hard. "I-I..."

The professor burst into a fresh wave of sobs. Something—or someone—had clearly terrified the woman.

Avery kept her voice low and comforting. "You're safe. Everything is going to be okay." She reached for the radio at her waist. "Madison to dispatch."

"Dispatch is a go."

"I need backup at the Fairman Building

ASAP. A medic too." She glanced behind her at the empty hallway. "The building is not clear. Responding units need to enter with caution."

Avery's gaze shifted to the stairwell. No one was there. She took off her jacket and wrapped it around the professor. The entire woman's body was trembling, and Avery feared she was going into shock. "Are you hurt, ma'am?"

"N-n-not me." Professor Jenkins grabbed her arm. The nails dug into her skin. "Upstairs c-c-classroom." Tears ran down her face. "She's...she's dead."

TWO

Texas Ranger Weston Donovan set his fishing pole in the back of his pickup truck next to the tackle box. He assessed the low-hanging clouds. Not a drop of late-morning sunshine poked through, and last night thunderstorms had ushered in a cold front. Perfect fishing weather.

A light drizzle peppered the brim of his cowboy hat as he lifted the tailgate and shoved it into place. Weston's cell phone rang. For half a heartbeat, he considered not answering it. Today was his first day off in over six weeks. Conducting back-to-back investigations had left him exhausted. Still, ignoring his phone wasn't a viable option. Weston was a lawman first. Everything else came second, including trips to his favorite fishing spot.

He freed the cell phone from his pocket. "Donovan."

"Hey, it's Luke."

Luke Tatum was a fellow ranger as well as Weston's good friend. They both worked together in Company A.

"Sorry to bother you," Luke continued, "but I have a favor to ask."

Weston leaned against his truck. "The last time you asked for a favor, I ended up spending months on a case. I was buried in paperwork."

"Don't be such a whiner. I was the one who got shot."

"Pssst, whatever. That was barely a scratch."

Downplaying Luke's near-death experience was a coping mechanism the whole ranger team used. None of them liked to think about how close they'd come to losing one of their own. Fortunately, Luke had survived. He was now married to his long-time love, Megan. They were expecting their first child any day.

"Before we get to the favor, how's Megan?" Weston asked.

"Actually, she's part of the reason I'm calling. Megan's gone into labor. I'm taking her to the hospital as we speak."

Weston straightened, his heart jumping into his throat. "Is she doing okay?"

"She's cool as a cucumber. I'm a nervous wreck." Luke blew out a breath. "Hold on."

There was some muffled conversation. A woman's voice—Megan's—floated over the line. It sounded like Luke was helping his wife into the truck. Weston's suspicions were confirmed when the sound of an engine rumbled to life.

"Ya still there?" Luke asked.

"Yes."

"Okay. There was a murder Friday night at Harrison University. The chief of police is a friend of Megan's. Her name is Avery Madison.

I need you to meet with her to discuss the case."

"Text me her number. I'll reach out to her after I hang up with you."

"Actually, she's on her way to your house. Avery was coming to meet with us and, clearly, that's not going to happen. Since she was already en route, it was easier to redirect her your way. Hold on, I'm putting you on speaker. Megs wants to talk to you."

"Weston, hey." Megan's voice was a touch breathy, but she sounded calm. "Listen, you've never met Avery, but I've worked with her several times. She's an outstanding police officer. Nothing much rattles her, but this...whatever happened Friday night has her shaken."

A patrol car turned on Weston's street bearing the Harrison University Police Department logo. It parked in front of his house.

"Don't worry about it, Megan," Weston said. "I'll take good care of your friend. You just focus on bringing a healthy baby into this world. I'll be saying prayers for you."

"Say a special one for Luke. He looks like he's about to pass out."

Weston chuckled. "Will do."

He hung up. Avery Madison, dressed in a police uniform, came up the driveway carrying a binder. Her strides were long and confident. A strand of copper-colored hair had freed itself from the tight bun at the nape of her neck. Damp from the rain, it flirted with the most piercing set of green eyes Weston had ever seen.

"Ranger Donovan?" she asked.

"That's me." He extended a hand. "Nice to meet you, ma'am."

"Ma'am is reserved for my grandmother and my subordinates. You can call me Avery."

She slipped her hand into his. Avery's grip was firm, her skin soft. The faint scent of wildflowers drifted across the space between them. A zap of something akin to attraction arced up his arm. It was immediately followed by stab of guilt. Weston dropped her hand. The wedding rings, hung from a chain around his neck, swayed under his shirt as he took a step back.

"Thank you for meeting me on such short notice." Avery's gaze slid to the back of the pickup and his fishing pole. "I'm sorry to interrupt your Sunday afternoon."

"It's not a problem." Weston led the way up the porch stairs, out of the rain, and gestured to a rocking chair. "Can I get you some coffee? Or water?"

"No, thank you." Avery sat. "Any more caffeine and I won't have to drive back to Harrison University. I'll be able to fly."

The chair seemed to swallow up her athletic frame. It wasn't that she was particularly small. Around 5'5", give or take, but the rocking chair had been made specifically for Weston. It'd been a decade since he'd played professional football, but he maintained a linebacker's physique.

He leaned against the porch railing. "Luke mentioned there was a murder Friday night at the university."

"Yes. A Caucasian female, mid-twenties, was found hanging in a classroom on campus." She removed a photograph from the binder and handed it to him. "I was the first officer on the scene."

Weston's gut clenched. Crime scene photos were never easy to look at, but this was particularly haunting. A woman dressed in a long white gown hung from the ceiling, a rope tied around her neck. Tilted over, under her bare feet, was a chair.

"Is she a student?" he asked.

"Don't know. No one from Harrison University, student or faculty, has been reported missing. As of now, she's a Jane Doe."

Avery's voice was weary, and for the first time, Weston noticed faint shadows under her eyes. Her joke about the caffeine probably wasn't far off the mark. Had she gotten any sleep since Friday night? If so, it'd been uneasy.

"As you can see from the crime scene photograph, at first blush, it appeared to be a suicide," Avery continued. "But evidence has ruled that possibility out. The coroner estimates the victim died at least 24 hours before she was found, and that classroom was used until seven p.m. on Friday evening."

Weston's gaze shot back to the photograph. His mind whirled. "The scene was staged."

"There's more. Around the woman's wrist was a handmade bracelet." Avery removed another photograph and passed it to him. The leather band had a charm threaded through it.

Weston frowned. "Is that a chess piece?"

"Yes. A pawn to be exact. And in the pocket of the victim's dress, there was a note." Avery flipped to a new page in her binder. Weston motioned for her to leave it in place and shifted so he could read the message. It was written by hand, in pen, using calligraphy-style letters.

The game begins, Avery, with the King's pawn opening.

. . .

It was signed The Chessmaster. Weston read the note once, then again. His blood ran cold. "The killer mentions you by name. Have you ever seen anything like this before?"

"No. I spent ten years with the Houston Police Department. First on patrol, then in the gang unit and homicide. None of the cases I've ever worked resembles anything like this." Her mouth tightened. "It's possible the killer singled me out because I'm the chief of police for the university."

Or it could be a threat. Weston knew it. Avery did, too, he was sure. Her face was a mask of professionalism, but he didn't miss the slight tremble of her fingers. There was no need to push the point. At least, not now.

"How many people know about the bracelet and the note?" he asked.

"A select few. We've been able to keep the murder quiet on campus for now, but it's only a matter of time before that changes. I'd like assistance on the case from you. I've worked with the Texas Rangers before. You're trained to handle high-profile cases, plus you get special priority at the state lab. Both of those things I need."

No doubt she would. Once word got out, there would be panic from students and parents. Not to mention the local townsfolk. But he had a feeling that wasn't why Avery had asked for his help. He glanced down at the photograph of the victim. "You're worried the killer may strike again."

"This crime isn't the work of an amateur. I looked up the phrasing he used in the note. A King's pawn opening is the first move in a chess game." Her jaw tightened. "So yes...I think this could be the start of something."

Her instincts mirrored his own. "Give me five minutes to change. Then I want to go with you to the university. I need to see the crime scene."

An hour later, Avery steered a golf cart across the main courtyard of campus. Harrison University, founded in 1870, was a small, public college built around a large quad. Many of the buildings couldn't be accessed by car. Weston was squeezed into the seat next to her.

Well-maintained flower beds lined the walkway. The fountain in the center of the courtyard sent up a spray of water.

"Nice campus," he remarked. "I imagine it's not always this quiet."

"No, it's busy during the week. We have roughly 3,000 students enrolled full-time and another 1,000 part-time, but only 600 live on campus." Avery maneuvered around the fountain and peeked at Weston out of the corner of her eye.

The man was heart-stoppingly handsome. Features so sharp and intensely masculine, they appeared chiseled out of granite. His dark hair was a bit too long at the collar and slightly shaggy on top, as if he hadn't had a haircut in a while. Weston's knees were practically touching his chest and his head was tilted to prevent smashing it against the roof. He held his cowboy hat in one massive hand. He couldn't be comfortable in the cart but didn't complain.

Although they'd never met, Avery knew a few things about him from her friend, Megan. Weston was widowed. A former football player. An excellent investigator and a good friend. Megan had hinted at setting Avery up with Weston a few times. Her friend was sure they would hit it off, but Avery resisted the idea.

Life was funny. A year and a half ago, Avery had been engaged and Megan had been the one rebuffing romance. Now the roles were entirely reversed. Her friend was happily married with a baby on the way and Avery was the one avoiding relationships.

"What kind of security do you have on campus?" Weston asked, cutting into her thoughts. "Surely, you have cameras."

"We do, but the security system is old and

outdated. Most of the cameras are focused on the parking lots. There are some on the pathways. When I took over as police chief six months ago, one of the first things I did was request money for a new system. The dean has been receptive to the idea—especially since we've had increasing reports of thefts on campus—but a new security system costs money."

"Let me guess, it's money they don't want to spend."

"Correct." She turned the steering wheel, following the path. "But, in all fairness, Harrison is a small university located in a tiny corner of Texas. Union County has only 2,000 permanent residents, not including students or faculty. Nothing like this has happened on campus before."

Weston grunted. "They fell into the common trap that serious crime only happens in the big city."

"Exactly. None of the cameras in the parking lots picked up anything suspicious, but

I have a theory about how the killer got into the building with Jane Doe's body."

Avery passed the main entrance to the Fairman Building and circled around to the side. A small swatch of grass was the only division between the building and a row of pine trees. She parked the cart and got out. Weston joined her.

"The Fairman Building is on the edge of campus." Avery pointed to a worn path leading through the trees. "Down that way is a public street. As a shortcut, students sometimes park there and come through the woods to the building. I believe the killer used the same method, bringing Jane Doe through this side door. He would've avoided any security cameras."

Weston frowned. "But it wouldn't have necessarily prevented him from running into someone. Another student coming out of the building or someone on the road."

"The victim was petite. The coroner found evidence indicating she may have been put into some kind of luggage. My guess is, the killer transported her in a large suitcase. I can't prove it because there was a huge thunderstorm that night and any tracks were washed away, but it's the simplest method. Students and faculty travel all of the time for various reasons. No one would've looked at him twice."

"It's a good theory." He eyed the side entrance. "Did you recover any prints off the door?"

"Nothing usable. There were tons inside the classroom where Jane was found, but that's not surprising considering the number of students passing through on any given day. I doubt we'll get a match to the killer. He's probably smart enough to have worn gloves."

Weston reached for the handle and pulled. The door opened. "Would this entrance have been unlocked on the night of the murder?"

"Most of the buildings, including this one, are open until ten o'clock at night. After that, students and faculty have to use their university IDs to gain access to any restricted area.

Each time an ID is scanned, it's stored in our computer system."

He gestured for her to pass through and lead the way to the classroom. "I take it no one scanned their ID prior to the discovery of the body."

"No, but it was only 10:30 when she was found, and the scene would've taken time to set up. It's likely the killer entered while the building was open." She paused. "How long do you think it will take to get an ID on Jane Doe?"

"Depends. I've already called the coroner's office and put a rush on it. If we're lucky, we could get an ID within a few hours."

Some of the knots in Avery's stomach loosened. She was grateful to have Weston's help on the case. More than grateful. He could've refused to take it on or asked her to wait. Texas Rangers were assigned a specific geographical area. Harrison University was in Luke's region, and technically, it was his case. But Weston had stepped forward to fill in without hesitation. No wonder Luke and Megan spoke so highly of him.

"Once inside, I think the killer used this set of stairs," Avery said, escorting Weston up one flight. "The classroom is right here."

The memory of finding Jane flashed before her eyes and Avery's hand tightened on the door handle. She took a deep breath. Someone had murdered the young woman, but he wasn't going to get away with it. Avery would do everything possible to get justice. She pushed open the door and stepped aside so Weston could enter.

"Who discovered the body?" he asked.

"Professor Marianne Jenkins. She called for a security escort and came downstairs to wait but realized she'd left her cell phone charger in her office. Once upstairs, she noticed the door to this classroom was cocked open, came to close it, and discovered Jane. As you can imagine, Professor Jenkins was terrified. She ran to the stairwell at the end of the hallway and tripped on the last couple of steps. That's where I found her."

"Was she injured?"

"Not seriously, but the poor woman had to be sedated. I was able to question her beforehand though. There were others in the building earlier in the evening, but to her knowledge, they all left around nine."

"And she didn't see or hear anything suspicious?"

"No. She was closed up in her office working for hours. It was her habit to play music to keep her company."

Weston was quiet for a moment. He wandered over to the windows and looked out at the courtyard below. "Why this specific room? There are classrooms on the first floor. We passed them to get up here. It would've been a lot easier to deposit Jane's body there. Or, even better, dump her in the trees. The killer went to a lot of trouble to stage the scene. None of this makes any sense unless we assume every action he made was purposefully done."

That same conclusion had haunted her all night. "Every action...including the note."

"Yes." He turned to face her. "Avery, if the killer merely wanted your attention, he only had to dump Jane's body on campus. You would've automatically been in charge of the case as chief of police."

Goosebumps broke out across her skin. "That's not what he did."

"No. He specifically targeted you in a personal note. Why?"

"I don't know." She rubbed her forehead. A pounding headache was blooming along the temples. One she knew would turn into a migraine later. "Like I mentioned earlier, I was with the Houston Police Department until moving home six months ago to work as Chief of Police for the university. None of the cases I've worked resemble anything like this. I've never been the victim of a crime. Never had a stalker. I can't imagine any way this could be about me."

"What about someone in your family? Have any of them been the victim of a crime?"

"No." She sucked in a breath and dropped her hand. "Oh, no. How could I have missed it? I'm not the only cop in the family. My father... he died fifteen years ago, but he was a detective with the sheriff's office. Maybe this isn't about me. At least, not directly."

Weston's mouth flattened. "Maybe it's about him."

THREE

Murder required patience.

The Chessmaster glanced over his shoulder. No one was in the hall. He ducked inside the classroom, careful to pull the blinds and keep the lights out. Most people were oblivious to their surroundings. He used that to his advantage.

On soft-soled shoes, he moved across the room toward the large bank of windows on the opposite side. Dusk had painted the campus with muted colors of blue and pink. The Chessmaster pulled a small set of binoculars from his pocket. He raised them, focusing on the Harrison University Police Department across the street, zeroing in on the third window from the left.

Avery Madison sat at her desk. Inside his gloves, the Chessmaster's fingers twitched. Rage churned his stomach and heated his blood. He longed to wrap his hands around her throat and squeeze the very breath from her. To watch the life drain from her eyes.

Not yet.

The Chessmaster took a deep breath. Patience. It was what separated the masters from the fools. Recklessness, poor attention to detail, selecting the wrong moment—these are what landed a man in jail. He did not make mistakes. No, he was vigilant and precise. Chess had taught him that. To strategize, to counter, to weigh his options and strike when the moment was right. Soon...soon Avery would know him.

More importantly, she would fear him.

He turned his binoculars to the large man in the visitor's chair. A glint of something pinned to the man's chest caught his eye, and he focused on it. A Texas Ranger's badge. Ahhh, Avery had called in the calvary, just as he'd anticipated. The Chessmaster shifted his attention to the man's face. No, it wasn't Luke Tatum. This man he'd never seen before. Never mind. The effect was the same. Avery had countered his move.

Time to advance the game.

FOUR

Avery adjusted the cool cloth on her forehead. Her headache from earlier was almost gone. Shadows stretched across her living room as the late afternoon gave way to evening. Cooper, her dog, placed his head on her lap and sighed. His fur was mostly white save for several large brown patches—one over each eye and another placed crookedly on his back.

She stroked his forehead. "Sorry we didn't get to go to the park today, but your mom had to work. I left you a bone. And there were squirrels to watch from the window."

His eyebrows shifted, and he gave another sigh. She'd adopted Cooper from the shelter shortly after moving to Union County. He was roughly five years old with all the attitude of a teenager and a propensity for chewing on shoes. Avery adored him.

"Fine." She scratched behind his ears. "Today wasn't great. But it wasn't for me either. I had to sit with a Texas Ranger for hours, answering a million questions about my life, searching for any possible reason a killer might've left a note for me."

They hadn't come up with anything. Which brought Avery right back to her father. Kenneth Madison had been an exemplary police officer, decorated several times for his service. The idea that one of the criminals he'd put away had circled back around to hurt her was unsettling.

Avery removed the cold cloth from her forehead and reached for the framed photograph on the end table. In the picture, Avery and her dad were sitting on the front porch swing. Kenneth was caught midlaugh, his smile wide and eyes twinkling. A faint hint of gray touched the hair at his temples. His arm was wrapped around Avery's shoulders. The love and adoration between them was captured in that one perfect moment.

Her grandmother had taken the photograph surreptitiously, and it was one of Avery's favorites. She'd been seventeen at the time. Her father died just a few months after the picture had been taken. Avery missed him every day.

Cooper shifted closer as if sensing her sadness and gently licked her hand. She stroked his head. "Thanks, Cooper. Love you too."

Her cell phone rang. It was her sister, Savannah. Avery answered. "Hey, sis."

"Hey. I'm checking on you. Nana's made enough chili for the entire town. There's also cornbread and chocolate cake. Please tell me you're still coming to dinner."

Avery chuckled. Her grandmother had a tendency to go overboard for Sunday dinner.

"There's no way I'd pass up Nana's chili. Set a place for me."

"Will do."

She grabbed the photograph, intending to return it to the end table, but paused. Avery's father had been a disciplined detective and meticulous notetaker. Every case he worked started with handwritten impressions, which were memorialized later into written police reports. "Hey, Savannah, do you know if Nana still has those notebooks Dad used for work?"

"I'd have to look in the attic to be sure, but I'm almost positive Nana threw them out years ago. I found a few of Dad's coats in the upstairs closet. There was a notebook tucked in the pocket of one, but I tossed it."

Her heart sank. "What about the coats?"

"We sold them at the church garage sale. Why are you asking for Dad's notebooks?"

Avery hesitated. "It's for a case."

"Is this about the murder at the university —" Savannah stopped and then huffed out a breath. "Nope. Forget I asked. Active investigation. You can't tell me anything."

No, she couldn't. The university was being very careful about what information was shared. Avery set the photograph on the end table and got up from the couch. Cooper groaned and stretched before following her down the hall to the bedroom.

"I heard on the news this evening that you brought in the Texas Rangers," Savannah said. "You aren't working with Luke on this, are you? I thought you told me Megan went into labor."

"She did. And before you ask, I haven't heard anything about the baby yet. As for the case, another ranger is working with me. Weston Donovan. He's very nice and has an excellent reputation."

He was also handsome and smart, but Avery wasn't about to share those qualities. Not even with her sister. Avery picked up a brush from her dresser and ran it through her hair.

"Where have I heard that name before?"

Savannah asked. "Wait. Isn't Weston the guy Megan was trying to set you up with?"

"Don't start, sis. Weston and I are working together. Besides, I'm not interested in dating. Which is exactly what I told Megan."

"Not every guy is like Jeffrey, Avery."

She winced thinking of her ex-fiancé, Jeffrey Strikes. He was a prosecutor, and they'd met while she was a homicide detective with the Houston Police Department. Avery had foolishly thought they were in love, until she walked in on Jeffrey fooling around with a junior attorney on his staff. The cheating had been devastating, and she'd broken off their engagement. But the bigger problem was grappling with her knowledge of the affair. Jeffrey's junior attorney was a subordinate. Having a relationship with her was against department policy.

Ultimately, Avery informed Jeffrey that if he ended the liaison, she would keep silent. Instead of taking her advice, Jeffrey counterpunched. He went to Avery's boss and said *she* was cheating on *him* with a subordinate officer. His accusation set off an Internal Affairs investigation and nearly ruined her career. Avery's name had eventually been cleared, but the entire experience had taken a toll on her.

"I know what Jeffery did was horrible," Savannah continued. "And he hurt you deeply. But there are good men out there. Honest ones. I don't want you to close yourself off to the opportunity for happiness if God places someone in your life."

"I hear what you're saying, but I'm just not ready. And dating someone I'm working with is never going to happen again." She set the brush down. "Let me finish getting ready. I'll see you in a bit."

Avery hung up. Cooper growled, drawing her attention. The dog was standing at the bedroom window. He'd parted the curtains with his nose and was staring at something. Avery joined him. The wide expanse of the grassy yard ended in a tree line.

"What is it, boy? What do you see?" She

waited a moment, her gaze flickering from one area of the yard to another. Shadows caressed the trees, but nothing moved. "I don't see a thing. Not even a squirrel."

She patted Cooper on the head before crossing the room and entering the bathroom. The mirror wasn't doing her any favors. Avery grimaced at her pale complexion and the circles shadowing her eyes. She splashed her face with cold water before digging out some makeup. A bit of lip gloss and a touch of mascara did wonders.

Cooper hadn't moved from the bedroom window. He stared intently at the glass and the yard beyond. Avery paused midstep. "Coop?"

He glanced at her before turning back to the window. He growled again. The hair on the back of Avery's neck stood up. Cooper wasn't a trained guard dog, but he also wasn't one to bark and growl at nothing either. Before she could even consciously decide, her feet were moving toward the nightstand. She slid open the small drawer. Inside was her Harrison University Police Department badge and weapon. Avery picked up the Glock 22, her fingers wrapping around the grip, and flipped off the bedroom lights. She let her eyes adjust to the darkness before moving back to the window and scanning the yard and the tree line, looking for anything that could've raised Cooper's suspicions.

There. Her heart skipped a beat. Was that a person? The shape was nothing more than a shadow. Still, her hand tightened on the gun. She quickly moved to the front door. Avery slipped on her work boots and a jacket to protect her from the cold. Cooper, sensing she'd finally listened to him, joined her.

"Sorry, bud, you have to stay here." The dog was more likely to put her in danger than save her from it.

She slipped onto the porch, plastering herself against the brick to avoid triggering the motion-sensor floodlights. The scent of wet grass and damp earth enveloped her. Keeping her gun pointed at the ground, she moved quickly toward the corner of the house. Avery's heart thumped hard against her rib cage, but her steps were sure and measured.

Using the house to provide cover, she peered into the woods. It was nearly dinnertime and the sun had set. The encroaching darkness deepened every minute as night took over. Leaves rustled and a shape moved.

"Police!" Avery raised her gun. "Come out with your hands in the air."

"Don't shoot me, Avery." Weston stepped out of the trees. "It'll create a whole lotta paperwork you don't want."

She lowered her weapon and struggled against the sudden wave of anger. "What are you doing sneaking around my backyard?"

"A perimeter check. Didn't you get my text message?"

"Clearly not, since I'm out here holding you at gunpoint." Her phone had beeped a few times earlier indicating some emails and text messages coming through, but Avery's headache had been so bad, she'd ignored them.

She pulled her shoulders back and glared at Weston. "You do realize I'm a trained police officer. You don't have to babysit me. We aren't even sure the killer is after me."

"True, but we aren't sure he *isn't* after you either."

Her jaw tightened. She wasn't in denial, but all they had was a note in a victim's pocket. It was weird and creepy—no doubt—but it also wasn't a clear threat. The Chessmaster could've addressed her simply because she was the university's chief of police.

"Listen, Avery." Weston adjusted the cowboy hat on his head. "Watching out for you has nothing to do with your abilities as a police officer. I know we've never met before today, but we both care about Luke and Megan. Which means—I think—that we could be friends. Friends look out for each other."

She took a deep breath. Part of her wanted to argue with him, but it would be hypocritical. Given the circumstances, if the shoe were on the other foot, she'd do the same. *Even the best cops need backup.* It was one of her father's favorite phrases. It was also one Avery lived by for her entire career. She couldn't stop now, just because it was inconvenient.

Avery relaxed her stance. "You're right. This case is unusual and it's smart to have someone watching my back. Although it'd be better if you didn't scare the life out of me in the process. Next time, give me a call before you start creeping around my yard."

"Sorry about that. I noticed you had a headache back at the office and I didn't want to wake you if you were resting." Weston met her gaze. "I promise. It won't happen again."

The last of Avery's anger melted away. Weston had scared her, and he should've called, but his reasons for sending a text message instead were thoughtful.

"Apology accepted." She paused, glancing at the trees behind Weston. "Did you notice anything suspicious during your perimeter check?"

"Actually, I did. Come with me."

Weston led Avery to a cluster of trees. He couldn't avoid sharing with her what he'd uncovered. She needed to know. Still, it wasn't easy. Avery handled herself with professionalism and a clear sense of duty, but she was also human. Being singled out by a killer had to be terrifying.

"Have you been out to this part of the property recently?" he asked.

"No, not this far back. I mow the lawn and tend to the flowers around the house, but that's it."

Weston pushed aside a low hanging tree bough and pointed toward a bush. "See how those branches are broken? The rain has washed away any footprints, but I think someone was hiding in here."

The scent of wildflowers drifted in the air as Avery moved past him to examine the area. Was it her shampoo or her perfume? The scent reminded him of warm, spring days on his family's ranch. Weston took in a deep breath before he caught himself. He had no business wondering about the fragrance she was wearing. Guilt rolled over him. It'd been five years since his wife's death from cancer. Yet the echo of his commitment still lingered, as real as the wedding rings hanging on the chain around his neck.

"There's nothing else to indicate a person was here. No cigarettes or trash." Avery fingered a broken twig. "An animal could've caused this."

"Normally, I would agree with you. Except those branches are broken in a strange way. And there's this." He joined her in the small space and let the bough he was holding fall into its regular position. "Now look."

Her face paled. "From here, someone would have a clear view of the back of my house. My living room. My..."

Bedroom. The thought sent a jolt of anger through Weston, and the vulnerability buried in Avery's voice only fueled his temper. She didn't deserve this. No one did.

Avery cleared her throat and lifted her chin. "Do you have a flashlight?"

He removed a tactical knife from his pocket and flipped on the flashlight attachment before handing it to her. She examined the broken bush more carefully. Then she moved to the area around it. "I don't know, Weston. This could be nothing. Like I said before, I've never had a stalker and I've never noticed anyone following me. And Cooper's never drawn my attention to anyone out here either."

"Cooper?"

"My dog. He's actually the one that alerted to your presence."

Weston rocked back on his heels. "I'm willing to acknowledge I could be completely wrong. My intention isn't to scare you, but I'm not going to withhold any information from you either."

"I wouldn't want you to." She handed the

flashlight back and lifted the branch. "Come on. Let's go inside. It's cold."

Weston followed her across the yard. Avery went up the porch, and when she opened the front door, a dog burst out of the house. Tail wagging and barking excitedly, he ran straight for Weston.

"You must be Cooper," Weston said, letting the animal sniff his hand. "Hey there."

Avery watched from the doorway. "He's great for letting me know someone's on the property, but he's not much of a guard dog. Cooper loves everyone."

Weston patted Cooper's head and the pup promptly lay down and exposed his belly. His tongue lolled out in bliss when Weston complied with the silent request. Avery shook her head. "What a baby you are, Cooper."

"He's great." Weston chuckled. "I love dogs."

"Do you have one?"

"No, traveling for work doesn't make it possible. One day."

He gave Cooper a final pat, then followed Avery into the house. It was a one-story with an open floor plan and decorated with comfort in mind. Family photographs were sprinkled around the living room. The walls were painted a soft blue and matched the throw pillows on the couch. The bookcase held rows of novels.

Avery yanked the curtains shut before turning to face him. She tucked a strand of silky hair behind her ear. "Did you actually go home this afternoon when our meeting ended?"

"I did, but the drive gave me a lot of time to think. It'll be easier to protect you and work this case if I'm in town, so I packed a bag and came back. I checked into the Sullivan Inn. Seems like a nice place."

"It is. Are you hungry? I'm supposed to have dinner at my grandmother's tonight. You're welcome to join us."

He was starving, but crashing a family dinner wasn't polite. "I don't want to impose—"

"Don't think twice about it. My grandmother loves having guests. It'll make her day." Her mouth twitched. "Besides, I know you're going to follow me over there anyway. I can't have you lurking around Nana's yard. My sister was in the Army for almost a decade. She'll spot you faster than I did."

He laughed. "That's a convincing argument. I've already had one Madison woman pointing a gun at me tonight. No need to make it two."

"Give me a few minutes to feed Cooper and then we can go."

"You got it."

Avery disappeared into the kitchen. Cooper followed along, tail wagging. Weston crossed to the window and moved the curtains to look into the yard. Nothing stirred. Was he wrong about someone being in the yard? His gut said no.

A King's pawn opening. That line from the note bothered him most of all. The killer was organized. Patient. He was also operating on some kind of plan. Leaving Avery alone was out of the question. Yet working this case would require coordinating with several law enforcement agencies, gathering evidence, and speaking to witnesses. Weston was smart enough to realize he couldn't be in multiple places at once. He needed help.

He took out his phone and dialed a familiar number.

FIVE

Later that evening, Avery shoved aside a collection of Christmas decorations and peered into the dark recesses of her grandmother's attic. The dim bulb above her cast long shadows. Framed paintings were stacked against the wall. Chances were her father's notebooks were long gone, but Avery wanted to be sure. She stepped farther into the attic toward a stack of unmarked boxes. Dust scattered in the air and she sneezed.

The stairs behind her creaked. Savannah, her older sister, appeared. They were two years apart but looked enough alike to be mistaken for twins. Both shared the same copper-colored hair, heart-shaped face, and green eyes. The physical traits came straight from their mother, who'd died when Avery was a year old.

Savannah paused on the last step. "Nana sent me to help you."

Avery used a knife to slice through the tape sealing the box and peeked inside. More Christmas decorations. "Weston still eating?"

"He's on his third bowl of chili. Nana is thrilled."

Avery chuckled. "Remember how much Dad loved her lasagna? He could eat a whole pan by himself. He and Grandpa used to fight over who was going to get the last piece."

Her sister laughed. "Poor Nana. You and I don't eat the same way."

"Thank goodness. I'd be two hundred pounds if I did." Avery opened another box. More decorations, but this time they were for Easter.

Savannah retrieved a roll of tape resting on

the windowsill. She used her fingernail to work up the edge. "Weston's nice. And he seems very smart. I know this case you're working is stressful and...well, I'm glad he's on your team."

"So am I." She paused. "Have you heard from Henry?"

Savannah's husband was in the Navy, and on his final deployment before his contract ended. After he got back, they planned to buy a house in town. Until then, Savannah was living with Nana.

"No, Henry hasn't called yet." Savannah blinked rapidly as of holding back tears. "I'm sure it doesn't mean anything..."

Avery abandoned the boxes and hugged her sister. "It's only been a few days since Henry left. You know how these things go. It can take a while to get situated and be able to call home."

"I know. I was a soldier. It's just hard to stop worrying." Savannah squeezed Avery before pulling back. Tear tracks lined her cheeks and her eyes were red. "I'm a mess. I have no idea what's wrong with me."

"You've never been on this side of a deployment before. You were always the one leaving."

"Ugh. I don't like it." She scrubbed her face with her palms. "Let's say a quick prayer for him."

The two women joined hands and prayed. It seemed to center Savannah, something Avery was thankful for. Afterward, they returned to opening boxes. None contained her father's notebooks. Savannah glanced at the stairs. "Come on. We shouldn't disappear for too long since we have a guest."

Her sister was right. It was rude to leave Weston. Avery held the final box closed while Savannah taped it, and then they went back downstairs.

The scent of warm chili and cornbread lingered in the kitchen. Nana was seated at the table with Weston. Approaching eighty-five, Marla Madison retained the echo of youthfulness. White hair, perfectly styled, accented her bright blue eyes and olive skin. Nana's hands were wrapped around a steaming mug of tea.

Weston was plowing through a chunk of chocolate cake. The fork looked like a children's toy in his massive hand. Avery noticed the tension in his shoulders had disappeared. For the first time since she'd met him this morning, he looked...relaxed.

"Hey." Weston lifted his fork and grinned. His dimpled flashed. "Hope you don't mind, but I couldn't resist diving in."

She felt herself grinning back. "Depends. How many slices of cake have you eaten?"

"That's his second one." Nana chuckled. "Good thing y'all came back when you did. Another ten minutes and there'd be no cake left."

Weston held up a finger to his mouth. "Shhhh. Don't give it away. There's still a chance they may leave again."

Avery stood in front of the chocolate cake on the counter, as if to guard it. "Not a chance, Ranger. You might be a guest, but dessert is where my manners end."

They all laughed. Avery cut a slice of cake for her sister, then packaged one for herself to go. She was still stuffed from dinner.

Nana took a sip of tea. "Did you find your father's notebooks?"

"No, ma'am." Avery pulled out a chair and joined them at the table. "Is there any other place they could be?"

Nana's brow wrinkled. "You could try the storage shed in the backyard. Not the one with my gardening supplies. The one your grandfather used for his tools. After Kenneth died, your grandpa kept some of his things, but I'm not sure what..."

Her voice trailed off and Avery's heart twisted. Nana and Pop had been married for almost sixty years. His death two years ago had been hard on her. Avery's dad had been their only child, which made the two grandchildren all the family Nana had left. It was one of the many reasons Avery and Savannah had decided to return home. Nana had helped raise them. They both wanted to support and be there for her.

"I'll take a quick look in the shed," Avery said. Finding the notebooks could unlock the case. It didn't make sense to wait. "Be right back."

Weston stood. "I'll come with you."

They grabbed their jackets and flashlights, heading out the back door. Nana lived in a neighborhood, but all of the properties consisted of two acres or more. The sheds were close to the fence line.

"You have a great family," Weston said.

"Thanks, I think so too." Grass crunched under Avery's shoes and her breath puffed out in front of her. "Sorry about all of the questions. Nana and Savannah could get jobs with the CIA as interrogators."

Weston chuckled. "I suppose it's only fair that I take a turn in the hot seat. I must've asked you dozens of personal questions today in your office."

He had. And Avery had to admit sharing so

much about her life with a stranger had been a bit off-putting. But Weston didn't feel like a stranger anymore. Over tonight's dinner she'd learned a lot about him. His father was a pilot, his mother a nurse. He had one younger sister. Weston had played football for most of his life, gaining a scholarship to college, then going professional right after graduation. Later, he joined law enforcement working his way to becoming a Texas Ranger.

They reached the shed. Avery retrieved the key from its hiding place under a nearby rock and opened the padlock. The doors creaked on their hinges. It smelled of wood chips and sawdust. She fumbled for the light switch and flipped it on. Tools sat precisely in their place on the peg board, frozen in time, as if waiting for her grandfather's return. Her heart twisted painfully.

Weston picked up a piece of wood. Half of it was whittled into an elephant. "This is beautiful work. His pieces are the one I saw in the living room."

"Yes. Grandpa was a carpenter. He liked to say it brought him closer to Jesus."

"That's a nice sentiment."

"I always thought so." Avery gestured to the cabinets. "If Grandpa kept my dad's notebooks, they'd be in there."

They dug around inside the storage shed and chatted. The conversation was light. Avery asked Weston about football and he had her in stitches discussing some of the antics of the coaches and players. Thirty minutes later, they hadn't found her father's notebooks.

Avery closed up the shed and locked it. The cold bit into her cheeks. "Thanks for helping me look."

"It was worth it." Weston elbowed her. "I got to regal you with my best stories."

"Confession time. I don't follow football at all, so I had to search for you on the internet. The few articles I read said you were excellent."

He shrugged. "It feels like a lifetime ago. But I enjoyed it. Running down the field, pushing yourself to the limits, and making a touchdown in front of a crowd...it's a unique experience. But law enforcement fits me better. It gives me purpose."

"My dad used to say it was a calling. I believe that."

"Me too."

His answer didn't surprise Avery, but hearing the words still touched something inside her. She felt a camaraderie with Weston. He understood how much she valued her job, because he placed the same importance on his.

They started back across the lawn. Weston shone his flashlight into the trees. "I'm going to say my goodbyes now. We'll stick to the plan. I'll do a perimeter check of the neighborhood and wait for you to leave, then follow you home."

They'd taken separate vehicles for this specific reason. Weston was hoping to flush out the killer. It wouldn't peg him for the murder, but catching him in the act of stalking Avery would give them a good starting point.

A cold wind fluttered a leaf across the grass. The night was inky black beyond the flashlight's beam. Was the killer out there? Was he watching? The hair on the back of her neck rose, but a steely resolve straightened her spine. If Weston's theory was correct, it was better for the killer to be hunting her than some other unsuspecting woman. Especially since Avery had Weston as backup.

Come and get me, you monster. Step out of the shadows and show us who you are.

If the killer was stalking Avery, he hadn't followed her to dinner.

Weston did two rounds of the neighborhood, then killed his headlights and let his truck drift to a stop on the side of the road where he had a clear view of the house. Wind snaked into the vehicle through the open window. In the distance, lightning blazed across the sky. More rain was coming. Somewhere an owl hooted and another answered.

His phone beeped with an incoming text message. He opened it and the image of a chubby-cheeked newborn filled his screen. Luke's baby. They'd named the beautiful little girl Ava Marie Tatum. Weston's mouth curved into a smile, but somewhere deep inside a jolt of pain ricocheted through him.

He sent a congratulatory message to Luke, then leaned his head against the back of his seat. His hand drifted to the chain around his neck. Weston pulled out the wedding rings from beneath his shirt. That initial jolt of pain spread into a familiar ache. Before Melissa was diagnosed, they'd talked about having a family. His finger traveled the edge of his wife's band. It was half the size of his own. Toward the end of her cancer treatment, Melissa had lost so much weight, she hadn't been able to wear it.

He missed her. Every day. It'd been five long years since Melissa's death. The loss had become hollower and more poignant with time.

Weston couldn't imagine moving on, falling in love, and getting married again. Yet a part of him yearned for a second chance at happiness.

The door to the house opened, and Weston tucked the wedding rings back inside his shirt. Avery appeared. She hugged her grandmother before strolling to her car. In her hand was a tinfoil-wrapped object. Probably her slice of chocolate cake. Weston's lips tipped up thinking of their teasing exchange in the kitchen.

Just as he pulled away from his hiding spot to follow Avery home, his cell phone rang. Luke's name flashed across the navigation screen. Weston hit the button on his steering wheel to accept the call from his fellow ranger. "Hey, man, congrats on your daughter. Love the name Ava Marie. How's Megan?"

"Getting some much deserved rest. Ava's being checked out by the doctor in the nursery, so I have a few minutes to talk. What's going on with Avery?"

Weston gave Luke a quick rundown of the

events. His fellow ranger listened carefully, only interrupting to ask questions for clarity. Avery's taillights glowed and her turn signal flashed. Weston mimicked her movements, keeping several car lengths behind. There wasn't much traffic this time of night, which made following her easier. It, unfortunately, also made his official state vehicle more noticeable.

"You believe the murder may be connected to Avery's dad?" Luke asked, once Weston was done talking.

"She thinks so. It's not a bad theory. Kenneth Madison worked for the Union County Sheriff's Department for over twenty years. Criminals tend to hold grudges, and if our killer was in jail, it's possible he's had a lot of time to plan and stew."

"I suppose. Seems to me, though, the most logical target is Avery. Have you asked about former boyfriends?"

"Absolutely. Her last serious relationship was with a prosecutor in Houston. His name is

Jeffrey Strikes, and they were engaged until last year." Although Avery hadn't provided many details, he sensed the relationship had been troubled. "Jeffrey was attending a conference at the time of the murder. Rock solid alibi. The few guys she dated in college have all moved on and gotten married."

"What about professionally? Cops make enemies."

"I'm not taking anything off the table. I've got investigators running down the people she's arrested, starting with the biggest cases first. I've also called Grady in for assistance."

Grady West was another ranger with Company A. The three of them—Weston, Luke, and Grady—were also good friends.

"I hate to drag him away from his family," Weston continued. Grady had a wife and two children. "But I don't see any way around it. I can't leave Avery alone and this case is bigger than I anticipated."

"No, you made the right call." Luke huffed out a breath. "Okay, let's say Avery is right and this is connected to her father. Kenneth Madison died fifteen years ago. Does the sheriff's department keep records that old?"

"Partially. If the case ended in a guilty plea or a conviction, it's been destroyed. However, if it's unsolved, they still have it. I've requested those files to be pulled. Trouble is, that leaves a lot of wiggle room. The killer could easily be overlooked." Rain sprinkled his windshield. Weston flipped on the wipers. "One of Kenneth's former partners, Mike Steel, is still a detective with the sheriff's department. Avery's reached out to him, but we haven't heard back yet."

"I'll contact some of the retired detectives I know in the area. Maybe something about this case will ring a bell with them."

"You just had a baby, Luke. Give the contacts to me—"

"Not a chance, Weston. Avery's my friend. And Megan's." Luke paused and seemed to realize his tone was harsher than he intended. He took a deep breath. "Making a few phone calls is easy enough to do from the hospital. Besides, these detectives know me. They're more likely to be candid if I speak to them."

"I appreciate it. Just don't mention the note. We're trying to keep it out of the media."

"Understood. I'll be discreet."

"Thanks, Luke."

He hung up. Avery took another turn and Weston followed. The street bordered the university, but on the opposite side of campus from the Fairman Building. Houses were on one side of the road and a thick row of trees lined the other, hiding the campus from view.

Suddenly, Avery pulled over and got out of her vehicle. Weston quickly closed the distance between them. She wouldn't have deviated from the plan if something wasn't wrong.

"What is it?" he asked, climbing out of his truck. The steady drizzle pelted his shoulders and ran off the brim of his cowboy hat.

Avery shrugged on a tactical jacket with the word POLICE placed on the back. "I saw a flashlight beam in the woods. I have to check it out. We've had several thefts on campus in the last few months. One was reported tonight in the last hour. A laptop taken from the library, which isn't far from here."

Weston didn't argue. As chief of police for the university, Avery was responsible for its safety. "Okay. Let's go."

He undid the snap on his holster but didn't draw his weapon. They couldn't be sure the person in the woods had a nefarious purpose. It could be a student taking a shortcut to the street from the university. Or a neighbor looking for a lost dog. There were any number of legitimate reasons someone could be tramping through the trees.

They crossed the street. The scent of pine and wet leaves mingled with the sound of the rain. Lightning flashed, illuminating the surrounding woods, and Weston spotted a figure dressed in a black raincoat. Judging from the height and build, the person was male.

"Excuse me, sir," Avery called out. "Campus police. I need to—"

The man spun. Something whistled past Weston's ear and thudded into the tree behind him. Bark exploded, tossing chunks into the air. A piece scraped his cheek.

He was shooting at them.

"Get down!" Weston flung himself at Avery, wrapping his arms protectively around her. They tumbled to the ground as more gunshots followed.

Avery cried out.

SIX

Weston's heart rate skyrocketed. Had Avery been hit? Another gunshot hit the tree next to them. He rolled, taking Avery with him, seeking shelter behind a large oak. A rock jabbed into Weston's ribs. He sucked in a sharp breath but ignored the pain, twisting his body to cover Avery's. One hand cradled her head; the other held her secure against his chest. Two more thumps followed.

Please, Lord, guide me. Help me keep Avery safe.

"Have you been shot?" Weston whispered in her ear. Warmth trickled over the hand buried in Avery's silky hair, fueling his worry. "You're bleeding."

"I'm fine. Scraped my head on a sharp stick. You hit?"

"No, he missed."

She pushed against his chest, turning her head in the direction the shots had come from. Weston belatedly realized his mistake. Avery wasn't a civilian. She was law enforcement and his equal. His instincts to protect her had overrode everything.

Weston eased away from her, pulling his weapon. He purposefully slowed his breathing to counteract the dose of adrenaline coursing through his veins. Beside him, Avery was doing the same. Her gun was in her hand and she scanned the surrounding woods.

"What's he doing?" she whispered.

"Calculating."

Either the shooter would stalk closer with

the intention of killing them or he would flee. The weight of that pressing decision stretched out. One breath. Two. Weston strained to listen for any sounds beyond the steady patter of the rain. He'd lost his hat somewhere in the attempt to save Avery from the shooter. Water dripped from his damp hair into his face.

The snap of a branch cut through the night. It was followed by footsteps moving away from them. Weston rose and glanced around the tree. The shooter was nothing more than a dark, moving shadow. He was heading for the street.

Weston bolted after him, knowing Avery would follow. Branches tore at his clothes and his boots slid on the damp pine needles. His heart thudded against his rib cage. Lightning flashed again followed by a roaring boom of thunder.

He drew up short. Where was the shooter?

Avery bumped into the back of him. Weston caught her arm just in time to keep her from falling. The sky opened up and the rain beat down on them. It flattened Weston's hair to his head and soaked his clothes. He swung his gaze from one end of the woods to the other, searching for the shooter.

The roar of an engine came from the street. Weston raced toward it. He burst out of the tree line in time to see a taillight fading into the distance. A motorcycle. The streetlights were bright enough he could make out a person on it, but not the license plate.

"Look." Avery pointed to the ground. A muddy tire track came from the trees and coursed along the grass divider to the street. "The shooter parked his motorcycle in the woods. This doesn't make sense. The thefts on campus have been problematic, but there's never been any indication the perpetrator was violent. At least, not until tonight."

Weston glanced down the street. Avery's vehicle, along with his, were several yards away. A sinking feeling settled in his chest. "Is this the route you normally take home from your grandmother's house?"

She sucked in a breath. Avery's mouth tightened and she nodded slowly. "It is."

Weston didn't have to say what he was thinking out loud. She already knew. It was written in the curve of her shoulders and the way her jaw tightened.

The shooter might not be connected to the thefts on campus. It could've been the killer, lying in wait.

For Avery.

An hour after the attack, the thunderstorm let up enough to collect forensic evidence from the shooting. Avery bent down to assess the water-logged tire track left in the grass. There was no way they would be able to pull a tire tread from it, and any footprints were also gone. That left them with only the bullets. Not much to go on.

She rubbed her forehead. The gash

hidden in her hair had stopped bleeding, but it'd left her with a mean headache. She was in desperate need of a hot shower, dry clothes, and painkillers. Two out of the three were impossible, but she had some ibuprofen in her car.

Half a dozen law enforcement vehicles crowded the street. The thunderstorm had kept curious neighbors at bay for a while, but once the rain stopped, they crowded around the crime scene tape. Several reporters had also arrived. Avery needed to make a statement for the cameras, but she had to make sure there wasn't blood in her hair first.

Was the shooter from tonight also the killer? A part of her wanted them to be the same person. The alternative was so much worse. If the killer and the shooter weren't the same person, then there were two madmen running around on campus.

Yet questions plagued her. Why would the killer leave a note on the victim if he only intended to shoot Avery as she drove home from

Nana's? And how could he be certain she would take that route?

Lord, help me find the answers I need to keep people safe. I don't want anyone else to get hurt.

Avery popped open the trunk of her vehicle. The red first aid kit beckoned. She rummaged around inside and located the bottle of painkillers, then dry swallowed two.

"You might try an ice pack as well," Weston said, coming around a patrol car.

He'd put a light jacket on, but his pants and boots were stained with mud. Avery's gaze locked on the scrape marring Weston's cheekbone. Her gut clenched. They'd recovered five bullets in the woods. One—the first shot fired—had missed Weston by a hair. He'd nearly been killed tonight.

Don't think about it.

"Ummm, I don't have time for an ice pack," Avery said. "The dean called. He wants me to make a statement to the media."

She rummaged around in her purse for a

makeup mirror and a brush, but couldn't find them. Not that they would help much. She probably looked like a drowned rat. Running her fingers through her hair, she gently tied it back into a low ponytail. She used a wet wipe to clean her face.

"Can you see any blood in my hair?" she asked.

Weston's gaze drifted across her face to the left side of her head. The look was so intense, it felt as physical as a touch. Avery's breath hitched. The scent of Weston's cologne—something warm and musky—mingled with the scent of the rain. She kept talking to distract herself. "I'm not great with the media. I hate being on camera and having reporters shout questions at me. But it's part of the job, you know?"

"I know. There's no blood in your hair. The rain washed it all away." He reached out and pulled something from the end of her ponytail. A pine needle. "There. Now you're camera ready. Or as camera ready as someone who was nearly shot an hour ago could be."

Her gaze drifted to the cut on his cheek. Guilt and responsibility tugged at her. She couldn't let it go. "Weston, just for the record. I'm sorry I dragged you into this. I know being a cop can be dangerous, but...this wasn't supposed to be your case. You're doing a favor and you nearly got shot in the process—"

"Don't. Don't apologize." His hand closed over her forearm, his touch warm and gentle. "None of this is your fault, and I'm thankful I was here to provide backup."

Their eyes caught and Avery's heart skipped a beat. She became immediately aware of the proximity of their bodies. One step forward and she would be pressed up against him. The memory of his arms cradling her as they fell to the ground, the way his hands protected her head, flashed in her mind.

It also sent off warning bells. Their fledgling friendship might've become cemented under a spray of bullets, but anything romantic was out of the question. Avery couldn't. Her last relationship had been with someone she worked with. It'd ended in unmitigated disaster, and she'd nearly lost her career in the process. She wouldn't make that mistake again.

Avery cleared her throat and took a step back, forcing Weston to drop his hand. "Okay, I'd better go do this."

He gave her a thumbs-up. She turned and strolled toward the crime scene tape and the bright camera lights. With every step, Avery's spine straightened. The reporters shouted questions at her with rapid-fire precision. She ignored them, raising a hand until everyone grew quiet.

"At approximately 9:00 p.m., dispatch sent out an alert that a student's laptop had been stolen from the university library," Avery said. She continued to give a brief overview of the events and provided a description of the perpetrator. "Anyone with knowledge of this crime is requested to contact the Harrison University

Police Department immediately. Thank you and good night."

She turned on her heel. The reporters' questions followed her, but she ignored them. A man stepped into her path. Around fifty, he had a full beard and wore dark-framed glasses. He shoved a phone in her face. "Chief Madison, how did it feel to be shot at?"

"What are you doing behind the crime scene tape?"

The reporter ignored her question. "Could this shooting have anything to do with the murder on campus last Friday?"

Avery tamped down her temper. It wouldn't be good for public relations if she lost it on a reporter. "Sir, you need to move back behind the yellow line. Now."

"Is it true the woman found murdered on campus was hanging in one of the classrooms? Did you believe it was a suicide at first? What changed your mind?"

"Sir, if you don't remove yourself from my crime scene, I'll have you arrested." She waved one of her men, Officer Samuels, over. "Escort this gentleman off the premises, please."

"This is a public street," the reporter huffed. "You can't remove me."

Avery stepped back. "Actually, sir, I can and I will."

"I'm a member of the press. My name is Greg Kilbourne of the Texas Tribute." Officer Samuels took his arm and Greg tried to pull away. "Let me go."

Avery was done playing nice. "Arrest Greg Kilbourne of the Texas Tribute if he causes you trouble."

The officer gave her a nod. "Yes, ma'am."

Out of the corner of her eye, Avery spotted Weston moving in their direction. His expression was thunderous. By his side was Detective Mike Steel of the Union County Sheriff's Department. Pushing fifty, Mike was dressed professionally in a business shirt and slacks, although the collar was undone at the top and he had no tie. His hair was turning gray at the temples.

Avery moved to intercept them. "Crisis averted, gentlemen. Stand down."

"First you get shot at. Then you give the reporters a hard time." Mike gave her a one-armed hug. Worry was in his eyes, but he plastered on a smile. "You sure are creating a ruckus tonight, kid."

The old term of endearment brought a small smile to her face. Mike and Avery's father had worked together at the sheriff's department. They'd even been partners for a while. As a result, Mike had known Avery since she was fifteen years old.

"Are you sure you don't need to go to the hospital?" Mike asked.

She wriggled out of his grasp before he jumped into protective mode. "I'm fine, Mike. The perpetrator never came close to hitting me."

Thanks to Weston. She passed a glance at him. The ranger was quietly watching their interaction and she had the feeling he was attempting to assess the relationship.

"Mike, have you met Texas Ranger Weston Donovan?" Avery took the opportunity to shift the conversation. "He was with me during the shooting and assisted. Weston, this is Detective Mike Steel. He's a family friend. Mike and my dad worked together for many years."

Weston nodded. "We met while you were doing the press conference."

"I've been assigned to take over the investigation into the thefts on campus," Mike said. "Shooting at fellow officers is something the sheriff's department takes very seriously."

"Good. I'm glad to have you on the team." Avery, like all of her subordinates, was a state officer. However, her jurisdiction ended at the campus border. Cooperating with local law enforcement was essential, and she'd been coordinating with the Union County Sheriff's Department about the thefts on campus for weeks. "Let me run you through what happened."

She explained the events in a clipped tone. Mike listened carefully, taking notes on a tablet and occasionally asking questions. When Avery was done, Mike turned to Weston. "Anything to add?"

He shook his head. "No, that covers it."

"This is a pretty extreme escalation for the perpetrator to take. It's not unheard of, but this isn't a high-crime area and the guy only stole a laptop." Mike frowned. "Is there any way this could be connected to the murder that happened on campus Friday night?"

"It's possible." Avery detailed the information they had on the murder. Mike's expression hardened when she described the note, although he said nothing. She also explained her theory about being singled out because of her father. "I called you earlier today, but you didn't answer. I was hoping to discuss the case with you."

"Sorry about not returning your call. My phone fell into a puddle of water. It's currently sitting in a bag of rice."

"Sorry to hear that." She grimaced. It didn't

sound like Mike's cell phone would make it. "Does the case sound familiar to you at all?"

"No, but that doesn't necessarily mean anything. Your dad and I were partners for only a few years. We could be looking at something Kenneth did as a rookie or toward the end of his career. Unfortunately, most of the men your dad worked closely with are either dead or retired. I assume you've done a search on murders following the same MO."

"We have. Nothing came up." Weston shoved his hands in his pockets. "Hangings are typical for suicide, but not murder. My guess is the perpetrator has killed before using a different method. Maybe strangulation by another means, which is more common and difficult to narrow down."

Mike nodded. "How long before we get ballistics back on the bullets recovered from tonight?"

"A couple of days. I've put a rush on them."

"And what about an ID on the murder victim?"

"The coroner's investigator is working on it," Weston said. "So far, no one from the university—student or faculty—has been reported missing and the victim's fingerprints didn't yield a result when we searched our initial round of databases. Interestingly enough, Jane Doe had a pacemaker—"

"But you said she was young. In her twenties, right?"

"Yep." Weston shrugged. "It's not common, but it does happen. We're tracing the serial number on the pacemaker. That should give us a name. I'm hoping it'll come through sometime tomorrow."

"If it does, let me know." Mike clicked his tablet closed. "Meanwhile, I'll keep some deputies on patrol outside your house, Avery, as well as the campus."

"Thanks, Mike."

"No problem. Nice to meet you, Weston."

Mike gave Avery another gentle hug before joining a group of deputies standing near the edge of the crime scene tape. Beyond the boundary, neighbors and persistent reporters still lingered. Avery scanned each face. Was the perpetrator mixed in with the crowd? Or was he long gone?

Either way, someone had shot at her tonight.

And she had no idea why.

SEVEN

Monday afternoon brought a fresh break in the case. Through the serial number on her pacemaker, Jane Doe was finally identified. Her real name was Debra Channing and she worked at the university as a janitor.

Weston stepped into the Harrison University Police Department. Officers spent most of their time on patrol, so only a handful of the desks inside were occupied. He nodded hello to a few people as he weaved toward the rear of the building. Avery's office was made of glass walls and the blinds were open.

Weston's steps slowed as he caught sight of Avery. She was seated at her desk. Her hair was pulled back at the sides, and tucked into a roll at the nape of her neck. With her sharply pressed uniform and polished badge, Avery was the epitome of professionalism. The average person looking at her would never suspect she'd been shot at the night before. Except Weston knew.

His heart fluttered. That nagging spark of attraction he'd felt from their first meeting reared back up, but this time, it was accompanied by a fierce protectiveness. Weston gave himself a mental shake. He liked Avery, but anything more than friendship was impossible. Even if—and that was a big if—he could consider dating again, it wouldn't be with a cop. Avery walked into danger, not away from it. It was her job, and a passion he shared, but his heart had suffered enough loss.

Weston knocked on the office door. Avery spotted him through the glass and waved him in but held up a finger, indicating he shouldn't talk. He took a seat in one of the visitor's chairs. A ringing came through the speaker from the phone on Avery's desk. It was followed by a generic voice-mail greeting.

"Hi, Professor Jenkins. This is Chief Avery Madison with HUPD. I stopped by your office this morning to check on you, but a colleague said you'd called in sick. Could you please call me back as soon as possible? I'd like to speak with you. Thanks."

"Is that Marianne Jenkins you were leaving a message for?" Weston asked.

She nodded. "Professor Jenkins was so upset on the night of the murder, she could only give me the basics. I was hoping to do a follow-up interview, maybe learn some new de-tails that could aid our investigation." Avery pushed away from her desk and stood. "Give me the rundown."

"I don't know much more than when we spoke this morning. The serial number on the pacemaker confirms our Jane Doe is Debra Channing. Twenty-three years old. Never arrested. Single. No children. Originally from Phoenix."

He opened the folder and pulled out a photograph of Debra, taken from her Arizona driver's license record. The young woman smiled shyly into the camera. She looked so young and hopeful. It was heartbreaking to realize that less than a year after the photo was taken, Debra had been brutally murdered.

Avery took it from him, studying the image carefully. "No one in Arizona has reported her missing?"

"No. Phoenix PD sent an officer to the address on her driver's license. The house is owned by Robert and Joy Channing. A neighbor explained the Channings were out of town on an anniversary cruise. He was able to confirm that Debra is their daughter. She moved to Texas about nine months ago."

"That corresponds with my records," Avery said. "Debra started working for the university about seven months ago. Robert Channing is listed as her emergency contact."

"I'm working on getting a search warrant for her rental house. We're also trying to locate the Channings for notification."

Avery winced. Weston shared the sentiment. The Channings were coming back from their happy vacation to the horrible news that their daughter had been murdered. Weston wasn't able to go back in time and stop her death, but he could get justice. He wouldn't stop until Debra's killer was behind bars.

"Okay." Avery handed the photograph back to him and circled the desk. "Let's see what Debra's manager has to say."

"What's his name?"

"Jorge Garcia. I'm familiar with him, because he cleans our department as well as the other administrative offices. Nice guy, and I believe we can count on him to be discreet. Still, I don't want to tell him she's dead, since we haven't notified the family yet."

"Agreed."

Finding out their daughter was murdered would be awful no matter what, but Weston didn't want the Channings discovering the information through news reports. They deserved better than that.

They found Jorge in the basement of the administrative buildings, organizing a supply room. Mid-fifties and heavyset, he sported a full beard, which contrasted sharply with his shaved head. Bleach stains spotted his blue coveralls.

"What can I do for you, Chief Madison?" Jorge's gaze jumped to Weston and then back to Avery.

"I need to speak to you regarding Debra Channing," Avery said. "When's the last time you saw or talked to her?"

"On Thursday evening." Before they could answer, Jorge stiffened. "It's her boyfriend, isn't it? Listen, I'm not just her boss. Debra is my goddaughter. If something has happened to her..." He inhaled sharply. "You wouldn't be here if she was okay. I heard about the murder on campus from the news, but...please, don't tell me it's Debra—"

He started to tip over. Weston grasped the older man's arm and directed him into a chair. Jorge sagged, like a balloon with the air let out. Avery went to the nearby water cooler and filled a cup. She handed it to Jorge. The man's hand was shaking so badly, some of the liquid spilled out and spattered his pants. He emptied the cup.

"Take a few deep breaths," Weston ordered. He didn't want Jorge passing out or going into shock. "I need you to answer my questions. It's important. Who is Debra's boyfriend?"

"His name is Victor Haas. They started dating shortly after he moved here. I knew the man was bad news the moment I laid eyes on him and told her so. But Debra was headstrong. And Victor could be charming when he wanted to be." He searched Weston's face. "Debra's dead, isn't she?"

"I'm sorry, sir. We can't say more. Debra's parents—"

"Are on a cruise. Yes, I know." He blinked

rapidly. "But if Debra was only injured, you would've said so."

Weston's heart sank. This was a hard aspect of his job—to maintain distance in the face of grief—but he had to focus on the case. "Why do you think Victor is bad news?"

Jorge's hand tightened around the plastic water cup, crumpling it. "For starters, I suspected he was using drugs. Victor showed up at Debra's house while I was there. He seemed high. I threatened to call the police and he left. Afterward, I tried talking to Debra about it, but she defended him."

Beside him, Avery started typing on her cell phone. Probably asking for local police to run Victor through the system.

"Was there anything else?" Weston asked.

"Yeah. He was abusing her. She came over to our house for dinner one night and my wife spotted bruises on her arm. It's not the first abusive boyfriend Debra's had. That's how she ended up in Texas. To get away from the last loser she was dating." Jorge let out a breath.

"We'd hoped working at the university would inspire her to go back to college."

"You said Thursday was the last time you spoke to Debra," Avery said. "Was it unusual to go so many days without talking or seeing each other?"

"We normally saw each other when she came to work, but Debra took some time off. She was going to San Antonio to visit a friend and clear her head. She told Victor it was over on Wednesday night. I was there. He took it well, but I should've realized..." Pain vibrated through Jorge's voice. "Victor was never going to let Debra go. I should've known what he was capable of."

Debra had broken up with her abusive boyfriend one day before she'd been murdered. Victor Haas was someone they needed to talk to. Now.

"How do we find him, Jorge?" Weston asked.

"Try the Grimes Hotel Apartments off the interstate. That's where he was staying."

Grimes Hotel Apartments was a sleazy estab-
lishment. It was a pay-as-you-go weekly room
rental, a hotbed of criminal activity including
drugs. Avery zipped up her jacket against the
evening chill. The parking lot smelled of urine.
Department of Public Safety patrol vehicles
created a barrier around Room 106. Victor's
room.

Weston came out of the hotel office and
crossed the parking lot to join her. "Victor isn't
here, but he hasn't checked out. We're arranging for a warrant so we can search the hotel
room. Should be coming through in the next
ten minutes or so."

"It's too bad none of his neighbors will answer the door. I'm sure one of them knows
where we can find him." She waved a hand
down the street toward a bar within walking
distance. "One of the troopers took a pass
through the bar. Victor wasn't there and no one
had ever heard of him before."

Weston rolled his eyes. "No surprise there."

Avery scrolled through his criminal record on her tablet. "Victor Haas is a real peach. He's been arrested for drug possession, theft, assault, and domestic battery. He did three years in prison for robbing a car mechanic shop." She frowned. "You know, the thefts on campus started after Debra and Victor started dating. Considering his criminal history, it's not a leap to think Victor might be involved. Did the manager of the hotel say what kind of vehicle Victor was driving?"

"No. In a place like this, no one knows nothing about nothing. But Victor does have a 2004 Ford Festiva registered in his name. We have a BOLO out on it."

BOLO was short for be-on-the-lookout. Every law enforcement officer in the state would be searching for his car.

Avery tapped her finger against the tablet. "Last night's shooter used a motorcycle to escape, but that doesn't exclude Victor as a suspect. He could've borrowed or even stolen it.

But I can't figure out any connection he may have to me."

"Nothing in his criminal record is familiar?" Weston asked.

"No. He was arrested once in Houston, but that was while I was in the academy. As far as I can tell, I've never come across Victor before this case." She pulled up Debra's photo on the tablet in an attempt to jog her memory, but nothing happened. Avery sighed. "Debra worked on campus for over six months, but I don't recognize her. I should've seen her before. Passed her in the halls, maybe said hello."

"And how many people does that happen with on a daily basis, Avery? There are over 3,000 students at Harrison University. Just students. That's not including faculty and staff. It's impossible for you to know each one of them."

Weston's argument was logical, but it did very little to assuage the guilt churning her insides. If she'd recognized Debra on the night of the murder, been able to identify her, then maybe Victor would be in custody now.

Avery flipped back to Victor's criminal record. "Maybe we were wrong and this case isn't personally connected to me at all."

"Too early to say yet. Victor grew up in this area. He may have crossed paths with your dad. Maybe as a juvenile." Weston glanced at the hotel. "Chances are, Victor didn't grow up in the best household. This could even be about a family member—Victor's mom or dad, even an older brother. I've got a fellow ranger of mine, Grady West, digging into it."

"I know Grady. Megan and Luke had a BBQ a few months back, and he was there along with his wife, Tara. She's very sweet. And their kids are adorable."

"They are." He pulled out his wallet and removed a piece of paper. "Maddy, Grady's daughter, loves drawing pictures for me. This is her latest masterpiece."

He unfolded the paper. The picture was done in crayon. One figure was huge—obviously Weston—holding the hand of a little girl on a sidewalk. They were both eating ice cream. Avery laughed. "You're the same size as the buildings."

"According to Maddy, that's why I'm not good at playing hide 'n' seek."

They laughed. Avery handed the drawing back to Weston and noticed a paper on the ground. It was stark white against the blacktop. Had it fallen from Weston's wallet when he pulled out Maddy's drawing? She bent to pick it up.

It wasn't a piece of paper. It was a photograph, creased and worn at the corners. She flipped it over. A beautiful, dark-haired woman smiled straight into the camera. The joy in her expression wasn't practiced or fake. It beamed out even though the picture was small.

"That's my wife," Weston said. His voice was soft, but there was a catch in his throat. "Melissa. She died five years ago. Cancer."

"She was beautiful. How did you meet her?"

He was quiet for a long moment and Avery's chest tightened. Maybe she'd overstepped the line. "Sorry. I don't mean to pry."

"No. It's okay. Melissa and I were in college together. She was smart and witty. A woman of deep faith. Kind-hearted and loyal. She came to every one of my football games. I quit when she got cancer to take care of her. After she died, I couldn't imagine being on a field knowing she wasn't in the stands."

A lump formed in Avery's throat. The way Weston talked about his wife touched her, and it spoke volumes about him. He was someone who stuck when things were hard. A man of character.

"After Melissa died, I was lost. I had money but no purpose. Grady convinced me to join law enforcement. It was my saving grace." Weston gently took the photograph from Avery's hand. "That whole part of my life—the football and my marriage—feels like a lifetime ago. Almost like it happened to someone else. Does that make any sense?"

"It does. You're a different person now. It's...it's like you want to move on, but you don't know how."

He tilted his head. "Spoken like a person who can relate."

She could. Avery had told Weston the bare basics about her ex-fiancé on the first day they met. While trying to narrow down the potential threat against her, they'd had to go through her former boyfriends. Not that there were many. Jeffrey had been her longest and most significant. But she hadn't gone into the specifics about why they'd broken up or the Internal Affairs investigation that followed.

She hugged her arms around herself. Just thinking about it made her sick to her stomach. What could she say? *My fiancé cheated on me. Blew up my life with a pack of lies and nearly destroyed my career to save face.* No. She did not want to discuss her ex. It was humiliating and reflected badly on her. How could she have been so stupid? How could she have fallen in love and gotten engaged to someone like Jeffrey?

A trooper across the parking lot gestured to them, saving Avery from having to say anything.

"The search warrant must've come through," Weston said. "Come on."

Avery fell into step beside him, snapping her mind back into professional mode. They went through the necessary procedures. Avery tugged on a set of latex gloves and entered Room 106.

It was a wreck. The bedding had been partially stripped and lay halfway off the bed. Clothes were strewn across the floor. The bedside lamp had been smashed. The closet door was cocked open, revealing several sets of shoes and a dirty backpack. Cigarette butts littered the small table next to the window.

She peeked in the bathroom. Towels and toilet paper mingled on the wet floor. Avery wrinkled her nose. "I can't tell if there was a struggle in here or if Victor is just a slob."

"Probably a bit of both." Weston pushed open the closet door. He stiffened.

"What?" Avery asked. "What is it?"

"Photographs. Of Debra."

She came up next to him and sucked in a sharp breath. Taped along the back wall of the closet were hundreds of photographs. Debra was in every single one, and it appeared they'd been taken without her knowledge. She was at the grocery store, a fast-food place, in the driveway of her home. Red marks crossed out her face in many of the pictures. Curse words had been scratched onto others.

It was the work of an obsessed man. And an enraged one.

Avery's phone rang. She yanked it from her pocket, barely taking her eyes off of the pictures to glance at the screen. It was her sister.

Avery answered. "I can't talk right now."

"Don't hang up." Savannah's voice was devoid of emotion and completely calm. It was her sister's military tone, shaped through almost a decade in the Army. She only used it in time of crisis. "Where are you? Are you with Weston?"

Avery locked down her own emotions, even as her mind ran through the worst. "Yes. I'm with Weston. What is it?"

Weston's head snapped in her direction. He stepped closer.

"I got off early today and picked up Cooper on my way home so he could spend some time with Nana." Savannah had a key to Avery's house and often took the dog if she had free time. Especially if Avery was working long hours. "Nana and I were bringing him back to your place when—" She took a deep breath. "I'm fine. So is Nana. We aren't hurt, but I need you to come home. Now. And bring Weston with you."

Her heart jumped into her throat. "What is it? What happened?"

"You need to get here, Avery. You need to see it for yourself."

EIGHT

Avery counted every mile to her house in heartbeats and prayers. The chatter from the police scanner in Weston's official vehicle increased her anxiety. Additional units had been requested. The neighborhood was being searched.

She gripped the handle over the passenger side window as Weston turned into the neighborhood. Half a dozen patrol cars were sitting in front of her home, along with several ambulances. Avery's stomach twisted. Did Savannah lie? Had something happened to Nana? A thousand possibilities flashed in her mind. She opened the truck door before Weston could come to a complete stop and jumped out.

"Avery, wait," Weston said.

She barely heard him as instinct overtook logic. She raced past the yellow crime scene tape. Mike stood in the driveway. His shirt was wrinkled and his hair was standing out in sharp spikes, as if he'd forgotten to comb it. He intercepted her, holding up his hands. "Your family is okay, kid. No one was hurt."

Weston came up beside her. Avery gestured to the vehicles in the street. "The ambulances—"

"A precaution. When Savannah called 911, they sent out EMS too." Mike met her gaze. "I promise. Your grandmother and Savannah aren't hurt."

She sucked in a deep breath and tried to calm her racing heart. "What happened?"

"The killer sent you another message." Mike shifted, revealing her front door.

A small pocket-sized notebook was stabbed

through and held in place with a large kitchen knife. The open pages fluttered in the crisp breeze.

Avery stepped forward. Her boots scraped against the steps. Familiar handwriting, illuminated by her porch light, stole her breath. "That's...that's one of my dad's notebooks."

"Savannah found it when she came to drop off your dog," Mike said. "Your grandmother was with her. They called the police immediately and then phoned you. Savannah didn't want to wait for responders out here in the dark. She did the smart thing, loading both the dog and Mrs. Madison into her car. They drove back to your grandmother's house."

Of course she had. Her sister was a soldier, used to combat. Although Savannah carried a concealed firearm, that didn't make her invincible, and her first priority would be getting Nana to safety. "Did they encounter the killer?"

"No. He was long gone by then. It doesn't

appear as though the killer went inside your house."

But he'd been on the property. If Savannah and Nana had arrived while he was still here... Avery let out a shuddering breath. "I should've warned Savannah and Nana not to come here."

"This isn't your fault," Weston said softly. She tore her attention away from the notebook and knife in her door. Red and blue turret lights flashed over Weston's face. His expression was grim. "Are you sure that's your dad's notebook?"

"It looks like his handwriting. Anyone have a set of gloves?"

Mike waved to a deputy who located several pairs. Avery slipped her set on. She edged closer to the door. Every step racketed up the tension inside her, but she locked down her emotions and focused on the task at hand. "Has this been photographed already?"

Mike nodded. "We left it in position for you and Weston to see."

"Appreciate it," Weston said. He'd joined

Avery on the porch, also wearing gloves. "What are you looking for?"

"I'd like to see how many pages are written on."

The knife had been shoved through the top cover of the notebook, along with several pages, but a majority of the sheets were hanging loose. She used the tip of her finger to flip through them. Definitely her father's handwriting. Only half the notebook was used.

She glanced at Weston. "I asked Savannah about Dad's notebooks. She thought they'd all been thrown out but also mentioned finding some of Dad's jackets. One had a notebook in the pocket. Savannah tossed the notebook in the trash, and the coats were sold at a yard sale months ago."

"So this notebook could be the one your sister threw away?"

"Yes. Another possibility is the killer was at the yard sale, and found another forgotten notebook in one of my father's jackets."

Both options twisted Avery's stomach. The

killer hadn't been stalking only her. He'd been watching her family too.

"No one will touch you or them, Avery," Weston said, seeming to come to the same conclusion. "We'll put your grandmother and sister under protection. Troopers will be assigned to watch over them 24/7 until we catch this guy."

"Avery, there's more you need to know," Mike said. "When responding officers arrived, they did a perimeter check of the property. A woman was hanging in the backyard from a tree. She's been murdered in the same way as Debra Channing."

Avery's legs turned to jelly. "Do you know who the victim is?"

"It's Marianne Jenkins."

Weston inhaled sharply. Avery closed her eyes as bile rose in the back of her throat. Professor Jenkins frightened face filled her mind. Had she seen something on the night of the murder on campus? Something that had made her the killer's next target? The questions ran rapid fire in Avery's mind as she tried to make sense of it all. "I want to see the crime scene."

Mike rubbed the back of his neck. "Avery, you don't have—"

"It's not negotiable, Mike." She stepped away from Weston and squared her shoulders. "Let's go."

Avery appreciated that Weston didn't try to talk her out of it. Instead, he fell into step beside her as Mike led them around the side of the house. They walked through the yard and into the woods. Floodlights had been set up around the crime scene. Part of a rope still dangled from a branch. Marianne Jenkins had been cut down and placed on a large tarp nearby. The coroner's investigator was making notes on a clipboard. They were a few meters from the hiding place Weston had found while doing a perimeter search on her property the other day. A shiver crept down Avery's spine.

"What do we know?" Weston asked. His voice was flat, and Avery recognized the ranger locking away his own emotions.

"She was hanging from here." Mike pointed at the short end of the rope tied around the branch. "Deputies said she was cold to the touch, so they didn't try to revive her."

"Any idea on time of death?" Avery asked.

Mike waved in the direction of the coroner's investigator. "John believes she was dead before she was hung on the tree."

"That's consistent with the first victim." Avery stepped closer to the tree. The branch was too tall for her, but Weston could easily reach it. So could Mike.

"Marianne is..." Avery's gaze darted to the woman lying on the tarp. "Was my height. This branch is tall enough she wouldn't reach the ground when the killer hung her. But an average man could still touch it easily."

"Probably why the killer chose it." Mike gestured to the street, a short distance away. "He likely parked over there and carried her to the tree. We found footprints in the dirt, although not good ones. We'll cast them anyway.

I've got deputies canvassing the neighbors, asking if anyone saw a vehicle in this area."

"He set the scene," Weston said. "Just like the first time. The killer placed her high enough to make it look like she'd hung herself, but he didn't want to run the risk she would survive. So he kills her ahead of time."

Avery nodded. She turned. She had an unimpeded view of her home. "From this position, I would've seen her when I stepped into the backyard. My father's notebook was left on the front doorstep to put me on alert. I would've immediately done a perimeter search and found Marianne."

She approached the tarp. Rope was wrapped around the professor's throat. Her legs and wrists were bruised. Nails on each of her hands were broken and blooded. Anger heated Avery's blood and her heart ached, but she pushed both feelings away. Every detail was important. Nothing could be overlooked. Marianne was dressed in the same white gown as Debra had been. Another consistency between the two crimes.

"Excuse me, John." Avery pointed at Marianne's hand, careful not to touch the body. By law, only the coroner's investigator had that right. "Could you check to see if she's wearing a bracelet?"

"Sure thing." He bent down and gently pushed up the sleeve of the nightgown.

A handmade leather bracelet was wrapped around Marianne's wrist. Dangling from it was a single charm. Avery bent down for a closer look and her breath stalled in her chest. "It's a rook."

"Check the pocket of the gown," Weston said.

John did as requested and pulled out a sliver of paper. He handed it to the Texas Ranger. Avery stood. She ignored the tremble in her legs. "What does it say?"

"'I've captured your rook, Avery. So far I'm winning the game. Hurry, hurry and make your next move. Time's running out.'" Weston lifted his gaze to meet hers. "It's signed The Chessmaster."

The murder of a second woman and the Chessmaster's note changed the case. Weston took every investigation seriously, but this was different. They were dealing with a serial killer.

Weston marched down the hospital halls, following the signs to the nursery. It was after midnight and visiting hours were long over, but an exception had been made since he was law enforcement. He stopped in front of the bank of windows separating him from the babies. A few of the beds were empty. Others held tiny bundles tightly wrapped in striped blankets.

A flash of color out of the corner of his eye caught Weston's attention. He turned. Luke Tatum was strolling toward him. From the looks of things, it'd been a long night. Luke's clothes were wrinkled and his hair was sticking up at all angles. Weston could relate. His own clothes were grass stained and he was bone-tired.

"Hey, Luke." Weston shook his friend's hand and clapped him on the back. "Congrats again on the baby. Which one is Ava?"

Luke pointed to a tiny bundle on the far right. A blue light was shining down on the baby. "Ava's right there. She's got jaundice, which is why she's under the special lamp. Nothing to be concerned about. She just needs a little extra care. Appreciate you coming down to the hospital to keep me in the loop on Avery's case."

"No problem. Grady and I have to meet anyway. At least this way, we get a sneak peek at the baby." Awful things had happened tonight, and a heavy weight rested on his shoulders, but Weston had learned long ago to embrace the moment. "Ava's beautiful, Luke. I'm happy for you."

"Thanks." He grinned but it faded. "We should discuss the case. Where's Avery?"

"She's with her grandmother, Marla, and

her sister. After the night they've had, Avery didn't want to leave them alone. A trooper is stationed outside their house and I'm staying in the guestroom from now on." Weston glanced down the hall. It was still empty, but he didn't want to have this conversation in the open. "Is there a place we can talk in private? Preferably someplace with coffee?"

They confiscated a break room after making arrangements with the nursing staff.

Couches ran along one wall. Weston sank into one and the springs creaked in protest. Luke poured them coffee. "Okay, start talking."

Weston filled Luke in on the evening's events, although keeping his tone professional took real work. He was both heartbroken and angry that Marianne Jenkins had died before they could save her.

His fellow ranger leaned back in his chair. "Is there any connection between Victor and Avery's father?"

"Not that we've found so far."

Luke's phone beeped. He unhooked it from

his waist and checked the message. "That's Grady. He's waiting at the nursery. Let me show him the baby and then I'll bring him in."

"Sure thing."

The door clicked behind him. Weston leaned his head against the couch. A thousand questions rolled through his mind. Why was the Chessmaster targeting Avery? How was he choosing his victims? The killer was on a mission and had a plan only he understood. To stop him, they had to act fast.

Lord, please guide me. Give me the strength and the wisdom to figure this out before another innocent woman is killed.

Voices filtered in through the closed door. Weston quickly added an Amen to his prayer seconds before his fellow rangers appeared.

Grady entered first. He carried a well-worn cowboy hat and his boots tapped against the tile floor. Weston rose to greet him. Luke bought some crackers from the vending machine and everyone got more coffee.

"I've brought Luke up to speed," Weston

said, jumping right back into business. He turned to Grady. "What did you find at Marianne Jenkins's house?"

He pulled a notepad from his shirt pocket and flipped it open. "The back door had been pried open and there were signs of a struggle in the bedroom. It appears the killer attacked her while she was sleeping. An initial search hasn't yielded any prints, other than the victim's. Chances are, the killer wore gloves. A neighbor reported seeing Marianne on Saturday afternoon, watering her plants, but she failed to show up to Sunday brunch with her friends."

"So the killer probably broke into her house sometime on Saturday evening," Weston said. "Was she killed there?"

Grady shook his head. "There's no sign Marianne was murdered in her home."

That matched with what they knew about Debra's murder. She hadn't been killed in her house either. Weston blew out a breath. "Did she have a home security system? Cameras?"

"Unfortunately not." Grady's mouth flattened into a thin line. "And no one reported seeing a strange vehicle parked in Marianne's driveway or in the neighborhood any time before or after the abduction."

"How does that compare to Debra Channing's murder?" Luke asked.

"It doesn't." Weston took another sip of coffee. "There were no signs of a break-in at Debra's house, nor were there any signs of a struggle. Her car was in the garage, purse and cell phone on the counter. It seemed she'd let the killer in, which brings us to Victor Haas. Her ex-boyfriend had a key to her place. Victor is still missing and no one has spotted his vehicle either."

Grady snagged one of Luke's crackers. "I've reviewed Victor's criminal record, and while it's substantial, nothing about it is particularly intelligent. He's the type to kill his girlfriend in a jealous rage, not plot out a complicated murder."

Weston nodded. "That's been bugging me

too. I could see him committing the thefts on campus, but both murders were calculated."

"They're also personal," Luke said. "The notes to Avery alone are worrisome, but nothing gets more personal than depositing a body on a cop's doorstep."

Weston's stomach clenched as the image of Marianne Jenkins flashed in his mind. He didn't want to imagine the fear and panic the woman had felt, but it was impossible to avoid. Worse yet was knowing the killer would strike again. And that Avery was in his sights.

Grady blew out a breath. "I reached out to Avery's ex-fiancé, Jeffrey Strikes, to do a follow-up interview. The alibi he provided for the night of Debra's murder is rock-solid."

"Yes, he was at a conference," Weston said.

"Correct, but I wanted to dig deeper to see if he could think of any possible suspects or leads. Jeffrey claims the reason he and Avery broke up was because she cheated on him. Avery had an impermissible relationship with a subordinate officer. Jeffrey says there was an Internal Affairs investigation."

Weston frowned. "That doesn't sound like Avery. At all." His gaze shot to Luke. "Did you know anything about this?"

He shook his head. "No. And I agree with you. That doesn't sound like Avery."

Grady leaned forward. "I could request the Internal Affairs record, Weston, but that'll take time. This may have nothing to do with the murders, but considering the circumstances, I think you need to question her again."

Weston's jaw tightened. "I intend to."

NINE

Morning sunshine filtered through Nana's lace curtains and splayed patterns on the kitchen tile. Avery stifled a yawn and poured herself another cup of coffee. Her eyelids felt gritty from a lack of sleep. The table was littered with the remnants from their breakfast. A plate had been set aside for Weston. Avery had heard him come in last night from his meeting with Luke and Grady around two in the morning, but they hadn't talked yet.

Packing a bag and spending the night at Nana's house had been the right thing to do.

Avery was especially glad to have Weston staying in the guest bedroom and a trooper stationed outside the house. But she worried about the killer's next move. Did the Chessmaster have a new victim already selected? What had happened to make him target Avery? It had to be something connected to her father, but what?

The back door opened and Savannah walked in. She'd taken the dog for a walk and was dressed for the cold weather in boots and a heavy jacket. A coffee mug was in her hand. Cooper raced in behind her. The dog's nose twitched and he bounced on his front feet. Avery laughed, snagging a small piece of bacon and tossing it to him. "Nana's spoiled you."

"He's the only great grandbaby she has at the moment. Spoiling is in order." Savannah shed her jacket, placed it on the back of a chair, and added coffee to her mug. "Nana ready yet?"

"Not yet." Their grandmother was going with Savannah to work today. Nana volunteered at the crisis center on a regular basis. "Weston has arranged for a trooper to follow you to and from work. Someone else will be stationed outside the crisis center. Still, I wish you would reconsider and stay home from work today."

The threats had, so far, been focused on Avery. But if her father was the catalyst for the killer's actions, the entire family was at risk. Avery wanted to ship them off to Siberia until this whole thing was over, but Savannah and Nana refused to go.

Savannah took a sip of coffee. "I can't leave the crisis center shorthanded. Especially not at this time of the year, when so many don't have heat. Volunteers are coming in to deliver blankets to vulnerable households. We have the elderly citizens' lunch meals. Plus the food drive in a few days. The items on my to-do list aren't something I can put off. People rely on the outreach."

"Why do you have to be such a do-gooder?"

Avery grumbled. "Why can't you hide out like a normal person?"

Her sister laughed. "Blame Dad. It's all his fault."

"I dare say, I also had a thing or two to do with it, young lady." Nana bustled into the kitchen on soft-soled shoes. She was dressed in a beautiful lilac sweater that made her blue eyes appear purple. "The women in my family are made of steel and faith."

Avery wrapped an arm around her grandmother. "True, but it would be nice if you were a little less gutsy sometimes."

Nana patted her cheek. "Pot meet kettle."

They all laughed. Nana and Savannah were shrugging on their jackets when Weston stepped into the kitchen. His hair was still damp from the shower and a button-down shirt molded over his broad shoulders. The scent of his aftershave drifted across the room. Avery's heart skipped a beat. It was ridiculous. He wasn't the first handsome man she'd ever worked with. Or been friends with. But the more time she spent with Weston, the more she liked him. It was a notion she didn't want to ponder too much.

"There you are, Weston. Did you sleep well?" Nana asked. "I hope the mattress was comfortable."

"Yes, ma'am. Very comfortable. Before you go—" He reached into his pocket and took out two business cards, handing one to Savannah and then Nana. "Written on the back is my cell, along with my colleague's, Grady West. If you need anything, call one of us. The troopers have been ordered to keep watch over you, but it doesn't hurt to have another means of communication."

"Absolutely." Savannah tucked the card in her purse. "I'll add the numbers to my speed-dial as well as Nana's."

The women left. Avery pulled down a mug and poured Weston some coffee. She jutted her chin at the plate on the stove. A mountain of scrambled eggs was buffeted by bacon and slices of toast. "We saved you some breakfast."

"Thanks." Weston patted Cooper on the head before bringing the plate to the table. "Join me, Avery. We need to talk."

The chair scraped against the tile as she sat down. "Did investigators find something during the search of Marianne's house?"

"That's not what I want to discuss. At least, not yet." He poked at the eggs with his fork before setting it down and pushing the plate away. "We need to talk about Jeffrey."

She reared back. "My ex? Why?"

"Grady contacted him for a follow-up interview. Jeffrey said you cheated on him with a subordinate officer and there was an Internal Affairs investigation conducted. I'm sorry, Avery, but I need to ask you some questions."

Personal questions. Invasive ones. Heat rose in her cheeks. Avery gave herself exactly three seconds to have a pity party. Then she took a deep breath and straightened her shoulders. Two women were dead. Whatever she was feeling didn't compare with that.

"Jeffrey told you half the truth." She took a

deep breath. "Let me start at the beginning. Jeffrey was a prosecutor with the District Attorney's office. I was a homicide detective. Dating isn't easy when you work in law enforcement. Cases take over and it's hard to maintain a personal life."

Weston nodded, following along, but said nothing.

"Jeffrey was charming and very smart," she continued. "He was fierce in the courtroom. It impressed me because it seemed we shared a passion for justice. We didn't date long before getting engaged, but afterward, things started to crumble. I wanted to move home. Living in a bigger city was great for jump-starting my career and to gain experience, but it was never my intention to stay there permanently. I wanted to be closer to Nana and Savannah. Jeffrey, however, was determined to stay in Houston. He had ambition and wanted to pursue politics. There was a lot of fighting, but I thought we loved each other and would work it out. Six months after we got engaged, I discovered Jeffrey was cheating on me with his junior attorney."

Her voice trembled and she fought to steady it. "I hadn't realized how calculating Jeffrey was until it was too late. He didn't care about truth and justice. He cared about appearances and had learned to say all the right things. Even his relationship with me was about strategy, not love. He wanted the right kind of woman to climb the ranks with."

The heat in her cheeks intensified as she recalled the angry words he'd flung her direction. In one fell swoop, Jeffrey's facade fell away, and it was humiliating to remember how she'd been bamboozled.

She traced the grain of wood in the table, unable to meet Weston's gaze. "I was devastated. Of course, the relationship was over, and I told him so. The real issue I grappled with was what to do with the information I'd learned. Jeffrey's junior attorney was a subordinate. Having a relationship with her was against department policy. I advised him to break things off and, if he did so, I would keep my mouth shut."

"Let me guess. That's not what happened."

"No. Jeffrey went to my superiors and claimed I was having an affair with one of my subordinates. His accusation nearly ruined my career."

————

The pain vibrating in Avery's voice was almost too much to bear. Her hair was pulled back in its customary bun, and she wore her police uniform, but the professional mask she'd perfected for work was gone. Sitting in the chair across from him wasn't a cop. It was a woman. A friend. And she was hurting.

Weston's fingers twitched. He longed to reach across the table and take her hand. To give Avery some small measure of comfort. He resisted. Although they were in her grandmother's kitchen, this was an interview. He had to maintain a level of professional distance.

Even if it hurt him to do so.

Weston pulled a small notebook out of his shirt pocket, along with a pen. "What happened after Jeffrey accused you of having an affair with your subordinate?"

"An Internal Affairs investigation was started, per department policy. The accusation was bogus, of course, but that didn't stop the rumors." Her hand tightened on the coffee mug. "The man Jeffrey named as my love interest, Scott Carpenter, was happily married with two children. I was labeled a home-wrecker. Colleagues were whispering behind my back."

"And because there was an active investigation, you couldn't defend yourself."

"Correct. Jeffrey was calculated in naming Scott. The officer had worked in my unit, but he'd left to pursue law school. Tracking him down for an interview took time. Which only dragged out the process and added fuel to the gossip. I was eventually cleared of any wrongdoing, but the damage had been done."

Weston didn't need her to explain why.

Police departments, even larger ones like in Houston, operated in many ways like a small town. Reputations were everything. Adding fuel to the fire was the fact that Avery was a woman. Weston had been in law enforcement long enough to know that sometimes his female counterparts were treated as less than. He didn't subscribe to the philosophy. His own superior and the leader of Company A, Lieutenant Vikki Rodriguez, was a woman.

"When the IA investigation was opened, did you share the information you'd learned about Jeffrey and his junior attorney?" Weston asked.

"I did, but Jeffery was prepared for that. Both he and the junior attorney lied. I don't think the investigators found any proof to support my claim. Which was the entire point, of course. Jeffrey lied about me, because it would discredit my own assertion about his affair. He did it to protect his career and neutralize any threat."

He tapped the pen against the paper. "Why didn't you tell me all of this?"

"Because Jeffrey had an alibi for Debra's murder. I didn't think it was important."

Weston nodded. "Still, we're going to dig more into your ex. Jeffrey is a District Attorney, so he knows the law and he's familiar with police investigations. He also holds grudges and he's got money. We could be looking at some kind of murder-for-hire situation."

"Weston, Jeffrey told Grady about the IA investigation out of spite. He wants to cloud my reputation and make you doubt my skills as a police officer. He's also a liar and a cheat. But I have a hard time believing Jeffrey would hire someone to commit these murders. He has very little to gain and an awful lot to lose."

"Understood. Jeffrey isn't my top suspect— it's Victor—but I also can't overlook anything." He paused. "I'll also have to check into Scott Carpenter's whereabouts. Just to eliminate him from the suspect list."

She licked her lips. "Can you do it personally? And quietly? I don't want to cause him any more trouble than Jeffrey already has."

"Absolutely. In the meantime, I've requested our behavior specialist take a look at the case."

Avery's forehead creased. "A profiler?"

"Yep. Her name is Emilia Sanchez. She's FBI trained and an outstanding investigator. Hopefully, she can give some insight into the type of perpetrator we're looking for. It'll take her a couple of days to put together a profile though."

Weston ran through the rest of what he'd learned last night. While he talked, Avery picked up his breakfast plate and popped it in the microwave. The scent of bacon made his stomach rumble. When she set the plate back down in front of him, Cooper rose from his bed in the corner and nudged Weston's arm.

"No, Coop." Avery shook a finger at the dog. "You've had enough bacon."

Weston chuckled as Cooper turned his big brown eyes on him. "Don't get me in trouble, pup." He patted the dog's head, then said a quick prayer before picking up his fork. "Avery, have you heard from Mike about your father's notebook?"

"He and I went over it last night. Dad would use one notebook until it was finished, so he often mixed cases together. Several were mentioned. One was a bar fight, another a hit-n-run, and a domestic battery. None of them seemed familiar to me. Mike's going to pull the files so we can look at them." She shrugged. "I'm not convinced the cases in the notebook mean anything. It's the connection to my dad that's important."

Weston took a bite of scrambled eggs. Even reheated, they were wonderful. "I'm inclined to agree, although we can't discount anything at the moment. Did you ask Savannah about the yard sale?"

"Yes. It was a church bazaar and was advertised in Union County and the surrounding areas. Tons of people came."

"So a lot of strangers."

Avery nodded. "Savannah doesn't re-member anyone with a particular interest in Dad's jackets, but she wasn't looking for any-thing suspicious at the time. Savannah did re-call selling different coats to several people, not just one, although she can't be sure to who. The event was months ago."

Another dead end. This case was full of them. Still, Weston would keep tracing any lead, no matter how small. There was no way to know which one would guide them to the killer.

Avery wrapped her hands around her coffee mug. "Why did the killer choose Mari-anne Jenkins as the second victim? Do you think she saw something on the night of the murder?"

"Maybe." Weston stabbed at a slice of bacon on his plate. "It also occurred to me the killer wanted Marianne to find Debra's body."

Avery bit her lip. "Maybe that's part of his pattern. Leaving the body for the next victim to find." She inhaled sharply, her gaze shooting to

Cooper. "Weston, we assumed the killer had left Marianne for me to find. But what if we're wrong. If he's been stalking my family, then he knows Savannah often takes Cooper in the afternoon and then brings him back in the evening."

He reached across the table and placed a hand on her arm. "I know, Avery. I thought of that last night and ordered a trooper be assigned specifically to your sister. We won't let the killer get close to her. And, keep in mind, I may be wrong. It's hard to say exactly what the killer's pattern is or how he's choosing his victims."

She nodded. "You're right. We've got a lot of questions and not many answers. Like why did the killer chose Debra and Marianne in the first place?"

"Exactly." Weston released her hand and picked up a slice of toast. "There aren't many similarities between the two women. They both worked at Harrison University and were single, but that's it. Marianne was in her 40s, white, divorced, and a professor. Debra was in her 20s, Hispanic, unmarried, and a janitor. They don't look alike. Debra didn't clean the Fairman Building where Marianne had her office. I have investigators talking to their families and friends, but nothing else has come up."

Avery frowned. "Mike and I looked in the sheriff's department database last night. Neither woman has a connection to my dad. While I knew Marianne Jenkins, it was only in passing. And I didn't know Debra at all."

"But somehow both of them caught the killer's attention. Why?"

"Well, the killer left my dad's notebook on the door for a reason. Victor Haas is our top suspect, which jives with the evidence. Debra knew the killer well enough to let him in. The missing link may be between Victor and my dad. Maybe I'll see something in Debra's house that will be familiar or jog my memory. Let's go there this morning and I can look around. We should call Mike and have him join us."

"It's worth a try. Inviting Mike along is a

good idea. Since he partnered with your dad for several years, something might jump out at him."

He polished off his breakfast and chased it with the last of his coffee while Avery loaded the dishwasher. But Weston kept turning over their discussion about Jeffrey. Their conversation outside the Grimes Hotel about moving on made a lot more sense now. It bothered him.

He stood and picked up his plate, bringing it over to the sink. "You didn't deserve what Jeffrey did to you. I hope you know that."

"I do." She reached for a towel to dry her hands but kept her gaze averted. "But no one forced me to date him. Or get engaged. I've been struggling with the fact that I was ever involved with Jeffrey in the first place, let alone so seriously. I'm a trained police officer. How could I have missed his true character?"

"Because you're human and we all make mistakes." Weston took a deep breath. This was a sensitive issue and he wanted to get the words just right. "When you learned about Jeffrey's cheating, you didn't try to destroy him or get even. He'd hurt you deeply. And you still treated him with fairness. Avery, you gave Jeffrey the chance to break things off with the junior attorney and put things right. Those are admirable actions. They speak far more about your character than anything else I've heard today."

Her breath hitched. She scanned his face, finally meeting his gaze. "I never thought of it like that before."

"Maybe you should."

TEN

Debra Channing's rental house was in a quiet neighborhood close to the university. The one-story would be classified as a fixer-upper in real estate terms. The shutters needed paint and weeds had taken over the flower beds. A broken tire swing dangled from a large oak tree in the front yard.

Avery dropped out of Weston's truck. Their conversation from this morning lingered, slipping into her thoughts. Weston's words had soothed a raw nerve. She'd been so busy berating herself over the relationship with Jeffrey, she hadn't considered an alternate view. One in which her core values—those of kindness and grace—had been used against her.

Weston circled the vehicle, settling his Stetson over his dark hair. Paired with the cowboy boots and the badge pinned to his shirt, he was the quintessential image of a Texas Ranger. Avery had never had a thing for cowboys, but Weston made her second-guess everything about herself.

"Mike's not here yet," Weston observed, bringing her attention back to where it belonged. On the case.

Avery unzipped her jacket pocket and checked her phone. "He sent me a message saying we should go on ahead. He's going to be a few minutes late. Do you have the code to the lockbox?"

Debra's rental house had already been searched, relevant evidence taken, and fingerprints collected. The property had been turned back over to the owner.

Weston nodded. "I've got the code. The

homeowner said Debra's parents are coming next week to clear the house out. We can come back as often as we need until then. She's not showing it to potential renters until next month."

They started up the drive. The rumble of a mail truck turning the corner caught her attention. Avery lifted a hand to shield her gaze from the sun. The man sitting behind the driver's seat was familiar. Mid-thirties with thinning blond hair and a gym rat's physique. Tom Bevin. His route covered her house as well as the police station on campus.

"Hey, Weston, give me a second. I want to talk to the mailman." She reversed course and Weston fell into step beside her. They were standing at the mailbox when the truck drove up. Avery greeted the man behind the wheel. "Hey there, Tom."

"Hi, Avery." He flashed her a bright smile before he seemed to realize which house she was standing in front of. His gaze flickered from her to Weston and then back again. "Suppose you want Debra Channing's mail."

"Figured I take it into the house." She gestured to Weston standing next to her. "This is Texas Ranger Weston Donovan."

"Pleasure." Tom shook his hand, then dug in the box next to him for Debra's mail. He handed the letters and a local grocery flyer to Avery. "I heard about the murder on the news. Shame what happened to Debra. She was a real nice lady."

"Did you know her?"

"We hung out a time or two. Nothing serious, but she was very sweet. Baked some cookies for me at Christmas time." He tapped a thumb against the steering wheel. "The family should put a stop hold on her mail. If you speak to them, could you mention it?"

"I will." She flipped through the letters. Nothing but bills. "Ever notice anyone in the neighborhood that didn't belong recently?"

Tom frowned. "No, but I spotted Debra's

ex-boyfriend a time or two in the neighborhood. Not at her house, just riding his motorcycle on the streets. His name is Victor Haas. I mentioned it to Debra because I know she was trying to stay away from him. He wasn't a nice guy."

Avery's heart picked up speed. The thief at the university who'd shot at them escaped on a motorcycle. "What kind of motorcycle does Victor have?"

"A Kawasaki Ninja. Black with green trim."

"Do you happen to know the license plate?"

"No, but you might check with Patrick Harpy, the owner of the gas station at the front of the neighborhood. I saw Victor filling up there...ummm, must've been Thursday afternoon." Tom glanced at his watch. "Hey, I gotta finish my route."

Avery stepped back. "Thanks for talking with us."

"No problem. And please don't forget to mention the stop mail to her family." Tom put the truck into gear and kept moving down the street.

Avery waited until he was out of hearing range. "We need to get camera footage from the gas station. Maybe it'll give us a plate number. If Victor does have a motorcycle, he could be the one who shot at us the other night."

"Agreed. I'll call Grady and have him pull it." Weston squinted at the house. "Trouble is, that doesn't tie Victor to the murders. And while he has motive for killing Debra—from all accounts, their relationship was abusive—I can't see why he would murder Marianne Jenkins. Or target you."

"Maybe he's trying to hide the real motive for Debra's murder?" Avery tapped the letters against her hand. "Victor's had some run-ins with the law. He knows his way around the system, and he's friendly with criminals. Killing Debra would immediately put him on the top of the suspect list. By staging the scene in the classroom, writing the notes, killing Marianne... that muddies the water and confuses the case."

"That's a lot of work just to create reasonable doubt. Far simpler to have an alibi. Still, it's worth considering. We'll keep following the evidence and have an open mind."

Weston and Avery followed the walkway around to the backyard. The gate was unlocked. Patches of dead grass fluttered in the cold air. The lock box was hanging from a water spigot and hidden behind a bush. Weston keyed in the code to retrieve the key and unlocked the back door.

The kitchen was neat. Open blinds allowed in plenty of sunlight. There wasn't a table, but two stools were tucked under the island. A water glass sat in the sink. Avery pulled out a pair of gloves and slipped them on. In case new evidence was uncovered, she didn't want to taint it.

Weston pulled out his phone, presumably to call Grady about the motorcycle. Avery tuned out the conversation and opened the fridge. Half a loaf of bread. A gallon of milk.

Condiments lined the door. Everything was neat and orderly.

She continued into the living room. It was sparsely furnished with a torn pleather couch and coffee table. No television, although there was a stand. Perhaps Debra had a TV in her bedroom. She wasn't making much money as a janitor for the university. A couple of self-help books littered the coffee table. *How to Gain Confidence, Getting the Love You Deserve,* and *Non-Abusive Communication.* Avery's heart ached reading the titles.

Several photographs had been hung on the wall. Debra posed with her younger sister and parents. Her smile was wide, her dark eyes sparkling. The ache in Avery's chest grew. While Debra had made a mistake in her relationship with Victor, it was obvious she was trying to set her life right.

Had Victor killed her for it? Or had Debra come across her murderer in another way?

Avery touched the young woman's face in

the nearest photograph. "I'll get to the truth. I promise."

She continued down the short hallway. A tiny bathroom was on the right. To the left was an office. It smelled of furniture polish. Avery opened the last door and stepped into a bedroom. The blinds were lifted, allowing an unobstructed view into the backyard, and a sliding door led to a small porch. On the bed, a lavender quilt was tangled with the sheets. A takeaway food container and drink carton littered the carpet. Half hidden under the bed was an orange backpack.

Avery frowned. One of the items reportedly stolen from the university in recent weeks was a similar backpack. She stepped farther into the room.

Air whirled as a figure, hidden behind the bedroom door, rushed forward. Avery half-spun, her hand flying to her weapon, but something heavy slammed into the side of her head. Stars exploded across her vision. Her fingers went limp and her knees hit the carpet with a bone-jarring thump.

Someone shoved her face down and straddled her. Panic welled, sending Avery's heart rate into overdrive. She thrashed, but the person holding her down was too heavy. Her mouth opened and only a squeak came out. No air. She couldn't pull enough oxygen into her lungs to scream. Out of the corner of her eye, the shadow of her assailant loomed above her. A man. But she couldn't make out his features. Blood dripped into her eyes.

The unmistakable feeling of a gun barrel pushed against the back of her skull. *Please. God, no.* He leaned down close to her ear, his breath hot against her cheek. "Don't move or I'll kill you."

His weight oozed the last of the air from her lungs and Avery feared she might pass out. The attacker's hand went to her waist. He yanked the handcuffs from her belt. Avery tried to fight back, in her mind she was yelling for Weston, but the knock to her head had slowed her responses. He secured her hands behind her back with the cuffs. The cold steel dug into the delicate skin at her wrists.

The gun returned to her head.

Weston heard a muffled noise coming from the rear of the house. He pulled the cell phone away from his ear, ignoring Grady who was giving orders for a trooper to gather the camera footage from the gas station.

"Avery?" he called out.

Silence answered him. A pinprick of unease jabbed the back of his neck. Weston glanced at the back door, focusing on the doorknob. The gold shine covering it was tarnished. Old. The owner hadn't changed the locks.

And Debra had either let the killer in, or he'd had a key.

Weston's hand went to his weapon even as he raised the phone back to his ear. "Grady, I think someone may be in Debra Channing's house with us. I heard a sound and Avery isn't answering."

"You think, or you know?"

"I think. Avery may have fallen or she may not have heard me call her name." He eased toward the doorway separating the kitchen from the living room. "Detective Mike Steel is supposed to meet us here. Get him on the radio and warn him. Send backup as well."

"Consider it done. I'm going to mute my side but leave the line open."

"Okay." Weston tucked the phone in his front shirt pocket. Keeping the line open enabled Grady to provide responding officers with vital information about what was happening in the house.

He peeked around the corner of the doorjamb. The living room was empty. Weston pulled his weapon from the holster but kept it pointed at the ground. If someone was in the house, there was a small chance the individual had every right to be there. He had no idea how many keys Debra had given out to friends or family. Weston and Avery might have startled or terrified the person.

He slipped into the living room, keeping his back along the wall. The windows faced the front of the house and the blinds were drawn tight. His boots whispered over the carpet. Weston's heart was beating like a jackhammer, but the hands holding his weapon were steady.

"Moving into the hallway," he whispered, for Grady's benefit.

He stopped and listened for any sound. Nothing. There was no reason for Avery to be so quiet. Something was definitely wrong. He wanted to rush down the hallway and get to her as fast as possible but battled back the urge. Weston couldn't be careless. He couldn't help Avery if he was dead.

Instead, he slipped down the dark hall. The first door was a bathroom. He turned in, leading with his weapon, checking to make sure it was empty. Water droplets sat in the sink, indicating it'd recently been used.

The door to the next room was open. An

office. Also empty. From the final bedroom, a muffled sound leaked out. It sounded like a suppressed scream. Weston's hands tightened on his weapon, and he took a deep breath, purposefully loosening his grip. He closed off his emotions, only allowing himself to rely on his training. Feelings could come later.

The door was cocked open. Weston edged up to the doorframe. He strained his ears but couldn't hear anything. With his boot, he kicked the door open. It banged against the wall. His breath caught as he raised his weapon.

Victor Haas was straddling Avery, holding a gun to her head. She was face down, her mouth smooshed against the carpet, preventing her from screaming. Blood coated the side of her face.

Victor flicked the gun in Weston's direction. Wood splintered as a bullet slammed into the molding.

Weston twisted out of the way, using the wall as cover. "Let Avery go, Victor Haas. It's over. The house is surrounded. You won't be able to escape the master bedroom. There's no place for you to go."

His instructions weren't just for Victor. They were for Grady too. By identifying the attacker, pinpointing their exact location in the house, and describing the hostage situation, it would aid backup officers. Weston prayed Grady could still hear him.

"You're lying," Victor shouted. "No one else is here."

The sound of glass shattering followed his words. Weston peeked around the edge of the doorjamb. Victor had broken the sliding door leading out to the patio. Probably with the butt of his gun. He held Avery upright and was using her body as a shield. It appeared her hands were bound behind her.

Somewhere deep inside, rage boiled, but Weston had to keep his head clear. He calculated his options. There weren't many. Best case scenario was stalling until backup arrived.

Weston ran into the bedroom, using a tall

dresser for cover. "Victor, you won't make it out of the backyard with her. Stop this now before it goes too far."

"I'm not going back to jail."

Weston's gaze shot to the backpack on the floor. He remembered reading a report about the thefts on campus. A similar backpack had been taken.

He peeked around the dresser. Victor was dragging Avery out the door. His hair was unwashed and his eyes wild. Under the influence of drugs, maybe? Some street drugs were known to cause superhuman strength. Weston wouldn't let Victor harm Avery more than he already had.

"Listen, stealing is small potatoes," Weston said. "I'm sure we can work out a deal. You won't have to go to prison. But if you hurt Avery, then things change. Everything is riding on the decision you make now."

He nearly choked on the lies, but they were necessary to keep Victor from escalating. The focus had to be on saving Avery.

Weston peeked around the dresser again. Victor was still in the same place. Half in and half out of the busted sliding glass door. Avery, however, seemed to have recovered somewhat from her head wound. When she met Weston's gaze, her eyes were clear.

She was calculating. Figuring out a move.

"Let Avery go, Victor, and we can talk some more." Weston shifted to the balls of his feet. "We can fix this. I promise."

The man wavered. Avery's head dropped, and then she reared up, slamming her skull into Victor's face. A resounding crack followed as Victor's nose broke. The man howled, releasing his hold on Avery. She dropped to the ground.

Weston sprang forward, jumping over Avery, and tackled Victor. The two men flew into the backyard. Victor's gun tumbled from his hand, landing somewhere in the grass. Weston vaguely registered Avery rushing over to the weapon as he wrestled Victor's arms behind his back and cuffed him.

"Get off me!" Victor hollered. "This is police brutality."

Weston had half a mind to shove Victor's face in the grass, but hauled the man to his feet instead.

Detective Mike Steel raced around the corner of the house. "I've got him."

Weston handed Victor over and hurried to find Avery. She was standing in the yard, leaning against the house. Smears of blood stained her hair and uniform. But she was alive. Emotion he couldn't describe mingled with the adrenaline, and Weston had the insane temptation to gather her in his arms and never let go.

As he approached, Avery's gaze slid from his. She turned and said, "Mind getting these off me?"

Handcuffs. Based on the empty spot on her utility belt, they were hers. Weston quickly undid them. "Come on. Let's get you to the hospital."

"Not yet." Avery turned to face Weston. She offered him a weak smile. "Nice tackle."

"Nice headbutt."

She lowered her forehead to his chest. Weston wrapped his arms around her. The yard filled with law enforcement. Dampness coated his shirt, and for a moment, he thought it was blood. Then Avery sniffled. She was crying.

He hugged her tighter, shielding her from anyone else's prying eyes. Weston didn't have to be told. He already knew Avery wouldn't want others to see her weep. That's why she hadn't wanted to go to the hospital right away. She needed a moment. "I've got you, Avery. I've got you."

"I know."

ELEVEN

The HUPD break room smelled like a mixture of stale pizza and dirty socks. Avery's nose wrinkled as she poured a cup of coffee. The sleeve of her uniform rode up. Red marks, left by the handcuffs, were embedded in her skin. It'd been twenty-four hours since Victor's assault, but the echo of her fear lingered. It sat in the center of Avery's chest, like a weight of cold granite.

Had Victor murdered Debra and Marianne? He'd demanded a lawyer after being arrested, which delayed questioning. She yanked down the sleeve of her uniform to cover the marks and doctored her coffee with hazelnut cream.

Jorge Garcia entered the room. His jumpsuit had his name embroidered on the pocket, and he pushed a large janitor's cart. "Hi, Chief Madison."

"Hello, Jorge." She took in his pale complexion. It didn't look like he was getting much sleep. Not surprising, considering his goddaughter had been murdered. "How are you?"

"I'm hanging in there. I heard about Victor's attack on the news last night..." He closed his eyes as if pained. "I'm thankful you weren't hurt badly."

"Thank you. I appreciate all of the time you spent answering questions about Debra. I know it can be tedious, but it's necessary."

Jorge had spoken to investigators several times since their initial conversation about Debra and her friends. He removed some antibacterial wipes from his cart. "I don't think I helped much. Debra didn't tell me a lot, probably because she didn't want anything to get back to her parents. Her mom and dad arrive in town tonight. I've arranged to take some time off to help them plan the funeral."

He blinked rapidly as if holding back tears, and Avery's heart wept for him and the rest of Debra's loved ones. She couldn't take away their pain, but she would do everything in her power to get them justice. "I'm sorry, Jorge. Please, call the station and let us know the funeral arrangements. I would like to attend, if I can, and I'm sure some of the other staff members would as well."

"That's very kind of you, ma'am."

He started wiping down the table. Avery topped off her coffee and went into the hall. Weston was waiting outside her office door, cowboy hat in hand. His dark hair had been trimmed. The haircut drew attention to the scrape on his forehead from tackling Victor and still-healing cut on his cheek from when they'd been shot at in the woods.

Their eyes met and that knot pressing

down on Avery's chest lightened. Her emotions were a tangled mess when it came to Weston. She wanted to keep him at arm's length, but it was impossible. Crying on him yesterday proved that.

"Hey, I was just coming to get you," Weston said. "Grady and Luke are here. They're waiting in the conference room."

"Let's go." She fell into step beside him. "You got a haircut. It looks good."

"Thanks." Dimples flashed in his cheeks, and her heart skittered. "Took only ten minutes at the university's salon. The stylist was a student in training, but I decided to risk it."

"You tackled a murder suspect yesterday. An inexperienced stylist is nothing compared to that."

He snorted. "Speak for yourself. I need a good haircut to offset my ugly face."

She chuckled. Weston could pose as a male model on any magazine in the country, but saying so would ruin the joke. "Sorry to tell you this, but the haircut doesn't help."

"Ouch."

They turned in to the conference room. The blinds were open, affording them a view of the flowerbeds and trees across the street. The wooden table was long enough to seat twelve, and a huge whiteboard took up one wall.

Luke rose from his chair at the table. He was clean-shaven, the faint scar at the corner of his mouth stretching as he greeted her with a smile. "Avery, it's good to see you."

"You too." They shared a brief hug. "Megan has sent me pictures of the baby. Ava's precious. Congrats. I'm so sorry you've been dragged into this case."

"Not at all. Megan and Ava are home now, and it's all hands on deck. Besides, Union County is close enough I can go home at night and see my family. Unfortunately, I also have a house guest." Luke threw a mock glare at Grady who was standing near the whiteboard. "He convinced my mother to make brownies and then ate every last one."

"That's a flat-out lie. Your beef is with your

wife. I only had two. The rest disappeared on her watch."

"Ooooohhh, you did not throw a new mom under the bus like that," Weston said, shaking his head. Avery joined in on the fun by crossing her arms over her chest and scowling.

Grady laughed and held up his hands. "I take it back. I'm the brownie thief."

The whole group laughed. Weston clapped each of his fellow Texas Rangers on the back and shook their hands. There were a few more jokes and good-natured teasing as everyone took their seats. It was clear to Avery the three men were very close and extremely supportive of each other. The warmth of their camaraderie was infectious, and it lifted her spirits.

The murders were terrifying and the case difficult, but there wasn't a better group of people to have on her team.

"Okay, let's get down to business," Grady said, opening a binder. "As you all know, Victor Haas immediately lawyered up. It took a bit of time to locate a defense attorney, and I finally interviewed him this morning."

Avery's palms were sweaty and she swiped them along her uniform pants. "Did he confess?"

"Victor admitted to the thefts on campus, as well as shooting at you and Weston on Sunday night. As for the murders, however, he claims to be innocent."

"Do you believe him?"

Grady's mouth pursed. "I wouldn't trust Victor farther than I can throw him. We had to offer him a sweetheart deal to get him to even talk to us. Normally, I wouldn't have done it—"

"Except we're on a ticking clock." Avery heard the anger and regret vibrating through Grady's voice. Victor would serve time for attacking Avery and Weston, along with the thefts, but it would be a fraction of the typical prison sentence given for these types of crimes. Sometimes deals had to be made to get to the truth. "If Victor isn't the Chessmaster, then someone else is. We need to know as soon as possible to have a chance to stop him. Don't worry, Grady. I know you did your best."

"She took the words right out of my mouth," Weston said. "Nothing is more important than preventing another woman's death."

"Thank you both." Grady gave a sharp nod. "While I don't take Victor at his word, his claims are supported by the evidence. Bullets shot from Victor's gun match those recovered from the shooting on Sunday night. A Kawasaki Ninja motorcycle was found in Debra's garage. Stolen from a man in Austin. According to Victor, he's been stealing laptops and cell phones from students on campus and pawning them to support a drug habit."

"What was he doing in Debra's house?" Weston asked.

"He was crashing there. Victor didn't have money to pay the hotel, news had broken about her murder, and he had a key to her house. He figured no one would be any wiser if he stayed there for a few days." Grady turned to face Avery. "Attacking you was a spontaneous decision. He hid when you and Weston arrived, hoping you would leave quickly."

"But then I went into the bedroom and saw the backpack on the floor."

He nodded. "Victor panicked. He has two felonies on record. Conviction for a third—like if you nailed him for robbery—would mean a long prison sentence. That's also why he shot at you on Sunday night. He didn't want to get caught with the laptop in his possession."

Avery tilted her head, mulling over the facts. "Shooting at us in the woods and attacking me in the bedroom were spontaneous acts. Victor hadn't planned them."

"No. Which fits with his criminal history. He's undisciplined. I don't think Victor is capable of orchestrating and carrying out a series of complicated murders."

Avery sat back in her chair. "So, Victor isn't the Chessmaster."

Weston mouth flattened into a grim line. "Which means the killer is still out there."

Weston had hoped Victor was the Chessmaster, but evidence didn't lie. For Avery's sake, as well as any other woman in the killer's path, they needed to move on. "I'd like to go over what we know about the murders, now that we can eliminate the shooting and the attack at Debra's house."

Grady nodded. "I figured you would. Our boss is coming in, along with the behavior specialist. I'd like to wait for them."

"Especially since they're bringing lunch from Sweet Hog." Luke joined a couple of fingers together and kissed the tips. "Best BBQ in Texas."

His antics pulled a small smile from Avery, but her complexion was pale. She pushed away from the table. "We have extra bottles of water and plasticware in the break room. I'll grab them."

"I'll help you." Weston followed her out of the conference room. He needed a moment to speak with her privately, before everyone else arrived. Luckily, when they stepped into the break room, it was empty. "Avery, hold on. I have more information about the case to share."

She tensed. "It's about Jeffrey."

"Yes. I did some digging. Jeffrey has a solid alibi for both murders. His financials are straightforward, so a murder-for-hire is out. I suspect you're right. He told us about the IA investigation just to discredit you."

Which only succeeded in making Weston hate the man. He hoped never to lay eyes on him.

"Scott Carpenter," he continued, "the man Jeffrey accused you of having an affair with, also has a solid alibi for both murders. Nothing indicates either of them had anything to do with this."

She leaned against the table and rubbed her forehead. "I don't know if I'm relieved or not. We're eliminating suspects right and left."

"I know, but meeting with the behavior

specialist and getting a profile of the killer should help."

"Thank you, Weston. For keeping your interview with Scott discreet."

"No need to thank me." He stepped closer, pulling the tactical knife from his pocket and clicking on the flashlight. Weston gently took Avery's chin in his hand and tilted her face up. "We're in this together. Flying bullets, tackling suspects, hunting a killer. Nothing boring about hanging out with you, Avery. Now do me a favor and stay still."

Her breath hitched. "What are you doing?"

"Checking for a delayed concussion. You've taken several knocks to the head in the last couple of days, and you're rubbing your forehead like a headache is brewing. I know the hospital cleared you yesterday, but concussions can develop later." He briefly shone the flashlight into each of her eyes. Her pupils were fine. Weston clicked off the flashlight. "Any dizziness? Or nausea?"

"No. I'm okay, Weston. Just a headache."

Their gazes met. There were flecks of gold buried in her green eyes. He'd never noticed them before now. Avery leaned closer and Weston's heart quickened. His thumb traced the delicate cleft in her chin. Her skin was soft. The scent of her wildflower fragrance wrapped around him, teasing his senses. Somewhere inside, someplace reasonable, Weston knew he should step back. But he couldn't get his feet to move.

Footsteps in the hall broke the moment. Weston released Avery and took a giant step back. Then another one. What was he doing? He'd almost kissed her. Maybe it was imagined, but the chain holding his wedding rings seemed to cut into the skin at his neck.

Avery's cheeks flushed and she spun away to grab water bottles from the fridge. An officer entered the room, carrying a takeaway bag from a fast food restaurant.

"Chief, more people arrived to see you," he said, pulling out a chair. "They went to the conference room."

"Thank you." Avery fished out some plasticware from a drawer and handed it to Weston. "We'd better hurry back."

The scents of BBQ sauce and fried okra
greeted them as they entered the conference
room. Weston plowed through the tender
brisket but barely tasted it. He'd perfected the
art of boxing off his emotions, but after almost
kissing Avery, it was difficult. The attraction
between them was like a constant buzzing,
flaring to the surface when he least expected,
and becoming impossible to resist. But this case
was complicated enough without adding romance into the equation.

Weston's boss, Lieutenant Vikki Rodriguez,
wiped her hands on a napkin. "Let's get started.
Grady has brought me up to date on the developments with Victor Haas, so no need to go
over it again. I've asked Emilia to focus on the
most relevant facts about the murders."

Emilia Sanchez rose and ran a hand down
the front of her pantsuit. Her dark hair was
pulled into a low ponytail. Weston had worked

174

with Emilia on several cases. She was highly intelligent and passionate about her work.

He closed the lid to his lunch and pushed it aside before taking out a notebook from his pocket along with a pen. Around the table, his colleagues did the same.

"There are three aspects to these murders I'd like to discuss," Emilia said. "The first is the bracelet charm placed on each victim's wrist. In Debra's case, it's a pawn. In Marianne's, a rook. The chess pieces have significance." She wrote on the board. "A pawn represents a peasant in medieval times. During a game, they're usually the first piece sacrificed."

"Debra Channing was a janitor here at the university," Avery said.

"Exactly. In our society, janitors aren't paid well. It's a menial job, which is why the killer chose Debra to be the pawn."

"What does a rook represent?" Lieutenant Rodriguez asked.

"It symbolizes the walls of a castle," Emilia answered. "Marianne Jenkins was posed at Avery's house for a reason. Her home was the castle, and the killer breached it."

The knot in Weston's stomach tightened. From the beginning, he'd suspected the killer was focused on Avery and now Emilia's observations confirmed the threat. "The notes addressed to Avery reference each chess piece."

"Yes. That's the second piece of evidence which I'd like to address." Emilia went to her binder and removed a piece of paper. "The note left on Debra's body reads 'The game begins, Avery, with the King's pawn opening.' The killer is letting Avery know he's started playing."

Beside him, Avery's expression was professionally blank, but under the table, her hands were knotted together. Weston leaned closer until their shoulders were touching. The urge to protect and comfort was instinctual and as impossible to resist as breathing.

"Playing?" Luke asked. "As in, the killer and Avery are playing some sick twisted version of chess."

Emilia nodded. "Chess is a game of strategy. Avery and the killer are opponents. This is supported by the second note, left on Marianne Jenkins's body. It reads 'I've captured your rook, Avery. So far I'm winning the game. Hurry, hurry and make your next move. Time's running out.' The killer is taunting her. He also seems to indicate she's made a move in the game, and he's countered by taking her rook."

"What kind of move did Avery make?" Weston asked.

"She brought you on the case."

Avery's brow furrowed. "But...if getting help from Weston triggered the killer to kill Marianne, that would mean everything I do is a move. Including this meeting."

Weston's gaze shot to Emilia who nodded. Her dark eyes reflected sympathy. "Yes. The killer is daring you to win the game—to find and stop him before he captures all the pieces on your board."

"And by capture," Lieutenant Rodriguez said, throwing down her pen. "You mean murder. Well, we aren't going to let that happen. You said there were three pieces of evidence. What's the third?"

"My father's notebook," Avery answered, before Emilia could speak. "The killer has targeted me because of my dad."

Luke held up a hand. "Hold on. We've dug through all of your father's arrest records and investigation files that we could find at the sheriff's department." He turned to Emilia. "And I've even contacted retired detectives who worked with Kenneth Madison. We can't find any case that's similar to these."

"I recommend you expand your search to assaults in which strangulation was used," Emilia said. "These murders are not the work of an amateur. Posing the bodies in the classroom and at Avery's house was risky. This killer is controlled, disciplined, and he's practiced in preparation for this competition. It's possible Kenneth Madison arrested the killer for a lesser crime—like assault—long ago. After that, the killer probably moved away, using distance and time to perfect his skills. But Avery is right. She's been targeted because of her father. The key is why."

"We can dig through the files again," Grady said. "Expanding the search to strangulations might yield new results."

Avery inhaled sharply and sat up straight. "I know another avenue to pursue. Calvin Miller is a retired FBI agent. He and my grandfather grew up together, but more importantly Calvin was a mentor for my dad."

Lieutenant Rodriguez nodded. "Good. Weston and Avery, interview Calvin Miller. Luke and Grady, look at strangulations in Union County. Focus on ones Kenneth Madison worked first and then branch out. In the meantime, Emilia, I want a complete workup of our killer. Race, gender, age, work experience. Everything."

Weston raised a hand to stop everyone from moving. "Emilia, how fast is the killer working? There were only two days between the first and second murders. We're beyond that now but no one has been reported missing. Yet."

"It's hard to say. He's smart enough to shift his plans based off increased police pressure, but it won't deter him for long. He's probably already selected each of his victims."

Beside him, Avery whispered, "The clock is ticking."

TWELVE

Nothing was better than murder, but a close second was planning the kill.

The Chessmaster hummed as he ironed the long white gown. The fabric was soft with lace detailing at the neck and hem. He draped the garment on a hanger before carrying it to the rear bedroom. Anticipation sank into him with fierce claws. The noose hanging in the center of the room, attached to a pulley system, stood empty. Everything was ready.

He opened the closet and hung the gown inside. Along the back wall was a collage of pictures arranged under printouts of different chess pieces. Avery was in the center. She was dressed in uniform, sunlight highlighting the curves of her face and copper-colored hair. The Chessmaster traced the line of her neck. Dark images fueled by twisted desires heated his blood. He wanted to hurt her. To make her pay for everything.

He closed his eyes and took a deep breath. Soon. Soon he would have Avery.

But not yet.

There was still work to do. Avery was a worthy opponent, but she hadn't figured out why they were playing the game. That moron Victor had interfered, causing confusion with his bumbling actions. He should've killed him. He still might.

The Chessmaster opened his eyes and scanned the photographs under each of the chess pieces. Victor's arrest would simplify things. Avery could focus on the right information, and that would help. But he couldn't risk any more delay. He wanted her to know. To understand.

To see him.

The Chessmaster's lips curved into a smile as he pulled a photograph down. There were basic rules and strategy, but each game of chess had its own unique signature. Avery had made her move by bringing on more Texas Rangers.

Now it was time to make his.

THIRTEEN

Late afternoon sunshine crept across Calvin Miller's ramshackle cabin. Firewood was piled on the corner of the porch, and a squirrel danced through the clearing to a collection of pine trees. Avery's breath created puffs in the cold air. She knocked on the wooden front door and shifted her feet to keep warm. It'd taken three hours to drive to this remote corner of Texas wilderness. She prayed it was time well spent.

Beside her, Weston shoved his hands in the pockets of his heavy jacket. "When you said

Calvin Miller lived off the grid, you weren't kidding. Does his house even have electricity?"

"Nope. He has a generator. Calvin never discussed it much but working as an FBI agent for four decades took its toll. This cabin was his escape from the world. When he retired, he moved here full-time. No landline. No cell phone. He goes into the nearest town for supplies and church on Sunday but otherwise stays here."

"How often did your dad visit?"

"Quite a bit. And I know they discussed work from time to time. I came fishing with my dad once or twice and overheard them." She knocked again before glancing in the smudged window. The inside of the cabin was dark. "I don't think he's here. Let's try the lake."

They stepped off the porch and she led Weston to a small dirt path. The scent of pine embraced them. Avery huddled deeper into her coat, even as her mind raced to fill the silence. The very awkward silence. Most of the car ride to Calvin's land had been spent discussing the case, but Avery kept replaying the moments from earlier in the break room. Even now, her fingers brushed against her chin. The sensation of Weston's touch seemed embedded in the skin.

She dropped her hand. Anything romantic between them was out of the question. Union County was Luke's area, but there could be occasions when Weston would assist on cases. Avery had vowed to keep her professional and personal life separate. She intended to keep that promise.

While Weston would never treat her the way Jeffrey had, that didn't eliminate potential complications between them. What if they dated but things didn't work out? Avery had enough sense to know a man like Weston wouldn't be easy to get over.

She needed to safeguard her heart. It was the only way.

A sudden break in the trees revealed a clearing with a small lake in the center. Calvin stood next to a nearby shack, holding a fishing pole in one hand and a pistol in the other. No doubt he'd heard them coming down the trail. Calvin was closing in on ninety, but his back was still ramrod straight and his mind as sharp as the hook on the end of his fishing line. He was dressed in a winter coat and waders. A thick beard covered the lower half of his face.

His eyes crinkled as a broad smile broke across his face. Calvin holstered the pistol. "Well, as I live and breathe, if it ain't Avery Madison."

She grinned and waved a hand at his waders. "I'd hug you, Calvin, but the car ride home won't be pleasant if I smell like fish."

He chuckled, but it ended in a harsh cough. Avery took in his flushed cheeks and surmised he was fighting off a cold. "It's not a great day for fishing."

"Gotta catch my dinner, Avery."

"Catfish?" Weston asked.

"Yep." Calvin's gaze swept over the Texas Ranger and narrowed. "You know anything about fishing, son?"

"More than a bit." Weston extended his hand and introduced himself. "Got another pole? I can lend a hand in catching your dinner."

Calvin hmphed but did as Weston asked. The group went to the lake's edge, and Avery waited until the bait was settled in the water before shifting the conversation to the case. She went through the facts they'd gathered and the connection to her father. "Do you know why someone might target me because of Dad?"

Calvin's jaw tightened. "Avery, is Mike Steel still working for the Union County Sheriff's Department?"

She frowned. "Yes."

"Then if I were you, I'd start looking at him."

Avery reared back. She would've been less surprised if Calvin had slapped her. "What are you talking about? Mike would never hurt anyone."

Calvin met her gaze before a tug on his line drew his attention back to the lake. "I never said anything before now because there was no need, but Mike Steel isn't the man you think he is."

"Stop talking in riddles, Calvin. Just say it."

He nodded and reeled in his line. A catfish plopped on the bank. "It started with an attempted murder. Beverly Wilson was in her home when a man broke in through the back door, assaulted her, and attempted to strangle her with a rope. The perpetrator was interrupted when Beverly's husband arrived home unexpectedly. Your father and Mike were assigned to work the case."

Avery's heart skittered. The basic facts—breaking in through the back door and strangulation with a rope—matched the cases they were working. Emilia had been right. They'd needed to expand their search of the sheriff's files to strangulations.

"Back in those days, the sheriff's department didn't have a crime scene unit," Calvin continued. "Kenneth and Mike collected the evidence themselves, and Mike was supposed to transport it to the lab. Instead, he stopped at a local bar. Mike had a drinking problem, but he'd contained it to his off-duty hours."

Weston pulled his own fish out of the lake. "Until he couldn't."

Calvin nodded. "Mike got drunk. While he was in the bar, his patrol car was stolen along with all of the evidence. It was never recovered."

Avery closed her eyes. "Beverly's case was compromised."

"That's right. Worse yet, Mike wanted Kenneth to cover for him by saying the patrol car was stolen while he was doing a safety check of the bar. Kenneth refused. He went straight to the sheriff and turned Mike in. The entire situation was an embarrassment to the department."

Weston groaned. "They covered it up."

"Essentially." Calvin tugged on the knit cap covering his hair. "The department made up a story about the stolen patrol car to save face. Mike went to rehab, but his career was irreparably damaged, and he blamed Kenneth. Mike's never been able to climb the ranks higher than detective because the stint in rehab went in his permanent file."

"Hold on," Avery said. "You're suggesting Mike killed two women and threatened me to get revenge for an incident that happened... what? More than twenty years ago? That doesn't make sense. I'm far more interested in Beverly's attacker."

"Except Beverly's attacker—guy by the name of John Starin—is dead. Kenneth kept working the case until he got a break. When the police went to John's house, the man opened fire. He was killed in a shoot-out."

Avery frowned. "Still, I have a hard time believing Mike is behind this. Drinking on the job is a far cry from murdering women."

Calvin threw his line back into the water. "I agree. It's extreme. But Avery, think about it in another way. You were a kid when Mike became a detective. Now, you outrank him and your career outshines his. Jealousy and revenge are powerful motivators, particularly when they've had decades to ferment."

A cold shudder ran down her spine. She didn't want to believe it, but...hadn't she also sensed Mike's jealousy? It'd slithered through their relationship since her move back to Union County.

Her heart skipped a beat. "Mike applied for the Chief of Police position at Harrison University. He mentioned it to me in passing once."

Weston's gaze shot to her. "When?"

"Right after I took the job. He came to the office to congratulate me and made a joke about how the job should've been his. It was awkward because I didn't know what to say. Mike never brought it up again, and I forgot about it."

"Avery, any job he applied to, the drinking incident would be reported to his potential new employer." Calvin arched his brows. "Losing the position to you may have been the final straw."

"He's triggered by it," Avery said. "Mike comes up with a plan of revenge, killing women in the same method as the case that started it all. Taunting me to catch him. Pitting us against each other…just like we were for the job."

Weston's headlights cut through the darkness as he took the exit for Union County. Beside him, Avery was quiet. The GPS was set for Mike Steel's house. Weston wasn't sure what to think of Calvin's assertions, but the sooner they confirmed or negated them, the better.

Weston's phone rang, his dash lighting up with Luke's name. Finally. His fellow ranger was tracking down the information Calvin had given them to verify it. Avery answered the call and let Luke know he was on speaker with both of them.

"Calvin was telling the truth about the fallout between Mike and Kenneth," Luke said, ignoring pleasantries. "According to the retired detective I spoke to, no one knew precisely why the two men stopped being partners. However, everyone in the department suspected it was connected to Mike's drinking. When he came back from rehab, many of the detectives refused to partner with him."

Weston flipped on his blinker and turned into Mike's neighborhood. "Well, that could create some resentment."

"What about the Beverly Wilson case?" Avery asked.

"The retired detective I spoke to remembered it. John Starin was the attacker. Beverly's necklace and her bloody nightgown were found inside John's house, along with a length of rope consistent with the one used on the victim. Kenneth was the one who closed the case."

"How did my dad figure out John Starin was Beverly's attacker if Mike's patrol car was stolen with all of the evidence?"

"Don't know," Luke replied. "I've requested the file from the sheriff's department, but it's apparently been misplaced. That's why it took me so long to call you."

"Misplaced, huh?" Weston asked. "Accidentally? Or intentionally?"

"Too early to say yet. The file room is a labyrinth and we're looking for a twenty-year-old case. I'll call you as soon as it's located."

Weston's hand tightened on the steering wheel. As a detective with the sheriff's department, Mike Steel had access to the file room. Had he hidden or destroyed the records? It was something to consider. "Thanks, Luke. Appreciate it."

"No problem."

Weston hung up. He stopped outside of Mike Steel's house and shoved the vehicle into Park. Avery was staring at the two-story structure, her mouth flattened into a grim line. "Let's do this."

They rang the bell, and moments later, Mike answered. He was dressed in sweatpants and a T-shirt, his hair disheveled. Behind him, a television was playing the news. "Avery. Weston. What are you doing here? Is everything okay?"

"No, Mike, it isn't," Avery said. "We need to talk."

Mike opened the door wider and let them pass. The living room was small and held a couch flanked by a couple of armchairs. A microwave dinner was balanced precariously on the corner of a portable table. Mike lowered the volume on the television. "Take a seat if you want. What's going on?"

"We have reason to believe Debra and Marianne's murders are connected to a case from a long time ago," Weston said. "One you worked with Avery's dad, Kenneth."

Mike's forehead wrinkled. "Which one?"

"Beverly Wilson."

The detective's friendly demeanor dropped away. He glared at them. "Beverly's case has nothing to do with these recent cases. Who told you about it?"

"That's not important—"

"Yes, it is." The tips of Mike's ears turned deep red. "I've worked hard to put my mistakes behind me, and now you've dredged them back up again. What game are you playing?"

"This is no game, Mike." Avery arched her brows. Game? Interesting choice of words. "When you heard about the circumstances surrounding Debra's murder, why didn't you mention Beverly Wilson's assault? The two cases are similar enough, you should've said something."

"Are you kidding? First of all, Beverly Wilson wasn't murdered. And second, her attacker is dead. John Starin isn't the one after you now. Not unless he's a ghost from the grave."

"How did my father figure out John Starin had attacked Beverly?"

Mike scoffed, tossing the remote on the coffee table. It landed with a clatter. "You think I know? I was in Arizona doing mandatory rehab for a drinking problem I didn't have."

"How long were you there?" she asked.

"What difference does it make? I'm not interested in revisiting ancient history." His gaze narrowed and he puffed out his chest. "I'll ask you again, what's this really about?"

Weston shifted until he was standing slightly in front of Avery, drawing the detective's attention back to him. "Where were you last Friday night between the hours of seven and midnight?"

Mike sucked in a sharp breath. He didn't answer. The color from the tips of his ears spread into his cheeks and neck. "I'm a suspect?"

The question came out through gritted teeth, and Weston had the distinct impression Mike was barely holding it together. He gestured to an armchair. "Sit down, Mike."

"This is my house. I'm not taking orders from you."

"If you like, we can take this down to the station for everyone to see." Weston kept his tone calm. "But I don't think that's in your interest. We aren't trying to take you down, Mike. Our goal is to get to the truth. Now sit down."

The detective threw himself into the chair.

He seemed to struggle with his emotions, his fingers clenching and unclenching. The man had a temper.

"I didn't have anything to do with the murders," Mike said. "Kenneth and I had a falling out, yes. And I was angry about the way he handled the stolen patrol car, but it's absurd to think I'd target Avery twenty years later because of it."

Weston decided to continue down that path instead of challenging him about the chief of police position at Harrison University. The point was to get as much information as possible. He sat in the other armchair and faced Mike. "We have to eliminate you now that this information has come to light. That's how investigations go, as you well know."

Mike's shoulders dropped. "It took me years to rebuild the trust of my department. How many people know about the stolen patrol car?"

"Myself, Avery, and one other ranger. That's it. Things don't need to go further, as long as you answer my questions. Where were you on Friday night between the hours of seven and midnight?"

"I was here." Mike laughed, but there was no real mirth. It came out hard. "Alone. My wife divorced me years ago."

Avery took a seat on the arm of the couch. From there, she could still listen in but wasn't in Mike's line of sight. Weston kept his gaze locked on the detective across from him. "What about on Saturday night?"

"I worked my shift. Got off in the evening at eight and came home. Went to sleep and returned to work for Sunday evening. And before you ask, no. No one can verify I was at home during the hours Marianne was abducted and killed." Mike blew out another breath. "Again, I have no reason to hurt Avery. This is ridiculous."

"Did you apply for the chief of police position at Harrison University?"

Mike's jaw tightened and his leg started bouncing. "I did. So?"

"It couldn't have been easy when Avery was hired for the job instead of you." Weston kept his attention on the other man, watching each facial expression as it flickered across his face. "Especially considering the history you had with her dad. I mean, if Kenneth hadn't turned you in all those years ago, if your time in rehab hadn't gone on your permanent record, you'd be in her shoes."

Mike froze, and a hardened mask dropped over his features. It was cold and unyielding, and a pinprick of fear stabbed at Weston. Had the enraged side of Mike, the out-of-control temper, been an act? Because the man Weston was looking at now was far different. This version of Mike could be responsible for two brutal, organized, and well-planned murders.

Mike stood. "We're done here. Get out of my house. Both of you."

Weston rose. "Don't be hasty—"

"I said get out. You don't have a shred of evidence linking me to these murders. If you want to interview me again, you can go through the sheriff and my lawyer." He pointed to the front door. "You know the way."

Avery's complexion was pale, but she squared her shoulders and turned for the door. Weston followed. The cold air smacked his cheeks. He glanced back inside to see Mike crossing the living room. Just as the detective reached to close the door, a car's headlights from the street swung into the living room. The beam flashed on a certificate hanging on the wall.

First place in the Texas State Chess Tournament.

Weston froze on the porch, that pinprick from earlier now a sharp jab. Mike shot him a hard smile before his gaze shifted to Avery. Something unreadable passed across his features.

Then he slammed the door in Weston's face.

FOURTEEN

Weston leaned away from his computer and rubbed his eyes. Almost eleven. For hours, he'd been digging into everything he could find about Detective Mike Steel and Jack Starin. It was a slow and frustrating process. Beverly Wilson's case file was still missing. Luke had assigned two troopers to search the sheriff's file room to find it.

Through the wood-and-glass doors leading to the small office nook, he spotted Avery pacing with her cell phone plastered to her ear. She was talking to the dean of Harrison University, and from the crinkle of her brow, the phone call wasn't going well.

Avery's grandmother appeared in the doorway. Her hair was tucked into rollers and she wore a belted robe. She carried a tray loaded down with a carafe and slices of pie. "I'm about to turn in, but I thought you and Avery would like a late-night snack."

He rose, took the tray from her hands, and placed it on the coffee table. "That's kind of you, Mrs. Madison. Thank you."

"Weston Donovan, if I've told you once, I've told you a thousand times. Call me Marla. Or Nana, if you prefer." The harshness of her words were softened by the look of affection she sent his way. "Anyone who saves my granddaughter's life has earned an honorary place in the family. I'm glad you're watching out for Avery."

"I'll do everything I can to keep her safe. That's a promise." He glanced at Avery, still pacing in the office. "Although I wish I could do more. This case is weighing on her."

Avery had been quiet for most of the day, and Weston knew she was hurting. Mike's potential involvement had taken things to a new, personal level. He was a family friend who'd eaten at their dinner table, sat next to them in church, and attended her father's funeral.

Marla tilted her head. "You help more than you realize, Weston. You're working together and sharing the burden. I know the case isn't moving as fast as either of you would like, but the Lord's timing is sometimes not our own. That's where prayer comes in."

"Yes, ma'am. I'll work on remembering that." Weston gestured to the pot of tea. "Would you like me to pour a cup so you can take one up to Savannah? She wasn't feeling well after dinner."

"No. I checked on her a little bit ago and she was out like a light. Her husband, Henry, finally called today. Savannah's had a lot of sleepless nights since his deployment. Hearing from Henry eased some of the worry she's been carrying around."

"I'm glad. I mentioned his deployment to my parents. They're keeping Henry in their prayers."

Weston had also asked them to pray for the entire Madison family. Every little bit helped. Marla said goodnight and shuffled out of the room. Cooper, Avery's dog, came to sniff the pie, but Weston shooed him away.

The door separating the living room from the office nook opened. Avery came in. She tossed her cell phone on the coffee table and collapsed on the couch. The familiar scent of her wildflower perfume tickled Weston's nose.

She leaned her head back and closed her eyes. "The dean refuses to cancel classes. He says there isn't enough proof the killer is targeting the university specifically and he's launching a new media blitz to counter the bad publicity. To make matters worse, we have the annual open house coming up this weekend."

"Open house?" Weston asked.

"It's a huge event the university holds every year. Prospective university students visit the campus. There are football games, theater performances, and parties." She opened her eyes and stared at the ceiling. "The dean sees money and future students. All I see are potential victims."

Pain vibrated in her voice. It didn't matter that Avery wasn't responsible for the killer's actions. Weston had come to realize she took the burden on herself. She cared. Deeply. It's what made her a great cop.

He slid his hand over hers, unable to resist the need to comfort her. "We're doing everything we can, Avery. I know none of this is easy for you. Especially now that Mike could be involved."

She bit her lip. "I keep turning it over and over in my mind. We haven't found anything connecting Mike to these murders."

"No, but he also aided in the investigation. Mike could've destroyed evidence and covered his tracks. Every step of the way, he's been informed of everything we know."

Avery hesitated, then leaned closer until

her head was resting on Weston's arm. A quiet stillness settled over them. Her hair was freed from its usual knot and flowed over her shoulders and down her back. It shimmered in the light from the end table. Her feet were bare, the toenails painted a pale pink.

The intimacy of the moment struck him. Weston considered ignoring the shift in their relationship but decided against it. Too much was left lingering since their near kiss yesterday. And he had a feeling Avery needed honesty and transparency in her life.

"I have to tell you something," Weston said. Heat climbed his cheeks. *Just say it, man. Rip off the Band-Aid.* "My feelings for you are growing beyond friendship."

She sighed, long and low. "I feel it too. I'd be lying if I said otherwise, but it scares me." She tilted her face to look into his. "The case has to take priority, and emotions are heightened. I don't want to mess things up between us. The timing is terrible—"

The vulnerability in her eyes made West-

on's chest tight. "Your grandmother just reminded me that God's timing is sometimes not
our own. Which is where prayer comes in."

"That sounds like her. It's good advice."

"It is. And, Avery, you aren't the only one
worried about messing things up." Weston
squeezed her hand gently. "I loved Melissa very
much, and although a part of me wants to move
on...I don't know if I have it in me."

Avery was quiet for a long moment, and
Weston was at a loss for words. He didn't want
to hurt Avery. Ever. But he wouldn't lie to her
either.

"So essentially, you and I both think this is
a terrible idea with bad timing and a question-
able outcome." Avery lifted her gaze to meet
his. "And yet, I can't manage to talk myself out
of it."

"Me either." Weston's gaze dropped to her
mouth. "Avery..."

She leaned forward, her hand coming up to
cup his jaw. Her thumb skimmed his lower lip
and the touch sent a wave of heat through him.

The desire in her eyes matched his own, and Weston was powerless to resist it. He closed the distance between them, and his heart rate skyrocketed as their mouths met.

Everything around them faded away, and Weston lost himself in the kiss. There was nothing but Avery. Her kindness, her bravery, her faith. Everything she was touched him and made him ache for more.

When the kiss ended, they were both breathless. Weston pulled Avery into his arms, and she rested her head on his chest. His heart was still beating a mile a minute. No doubt she could hear it. As his emotions settled, Weston braced himself for a pang of misgiving, the familiar sense of betrayal that had haunted his forward momentum with Avery. But it never came. Instead, a feeling of rightness settled over him. He didn't know what the future would bring, but Weston was grateful for this small moment.

Footsteps pounded over the hardwood seconds before Savannah came rushing into the living room. Her hair was mussed and her eyes wide. She had a cell phone in one hand.

Avery sprang from the couch. "What is it? Is it Henry?"

"No, it's one of my friends. Her dog was running around the yard and the back door is open. The neighbor said he's tried knocking several times, but Rachel won't come to the door. She's missing."

It took twenty minutes to drive across town to Rachel Long's house. Red and blue turret lights flashed from different patrol cars, casting patterns on the asphalt. The cold air stung Avery's lungs, and she kept an arm wrapped around Savannah's waist. Her sister's expression was pinched with worry.

Beside them, Weston walked protectively. Less than an hour ago, they'd been sharing a passionate kiss. Now they were at a crime scene. The twisting events served as a stark reminder for Avery to tread lightly. She didn't regret sharing the truth with Weston about her feelings, nor was she upset he'd shared his. But the conversation confirmed what she already knew. Her heart was in trouble of being broken.

Beyond the cordoned-off area, reporters shouted questions. Avery spotted a familiar face. Greg Kilbourne from the Texas Tribute. He was pushing against the barrier. "Chief, is Rachel the latest victim of the serial killer? Did the killer leave a note for you like he did with the other women?"

Avery froze, midstep. She glanced at Weston. "How did he find out about the notes?"

Weston's jaw tightened. "Mike?"

"Take Savannah up to the house. I'll be right there." She pressed her lips together and waved at a nearby officer to let Greg approach. The reporter rushed up, his tie flapping in the breeze of his own making. Avery didn't let him get in a question. "How do you know about the notes?"

Greg adjusted his dark-framed glasses. "I

can't reveal my sources, Chief. Are you confirming the notes are real?"

"I'm not confirming anything."

"They singled you out specifically." He glanced at the notepad in his hand. "Avery, the game begins with a King's pawn opening."

She stiffened. A selected number of people knew about the notes. And only one person benefited from cozying up to a reporter. Mike Steel. By feeding Greg information, he created a relationship that could be used later to cast doubt on his own guilt in the court of opinion. Avery cleared her throat. "Let's make a deal."

Greg lifted a bushy eyebrow and a gleam came into his eye. "I'm listening."

"I'll give you an exclusive one-on-one interview when this case is closed. You'll have access to inside information, and no question will be off-limits. In exchange, I want your word that you won't publish anything until I give my say so. Starting with the notes and their contents."

The reporter was silent for a long moment. "And if I don't agree?"

"I'll have you arrested for interfering with a police investigation. You'll get out of jail eventually, but do you really want to waste time in front of a judge?" She gestured to the other reporters. "Especially if it means one of them will get the scoop."

His gaze narrowed. "Fine. But I want some information now. I need something to keep my editor happy."

She pondered the offer. The dean wanted to put the university in a better light. This could kill two birds with one stone. "Meet me in my office tomorrow morning at ten a.m. You can interview me and the dean."

"Done."

She sent up a silent prayer that making a deal with the reporter was the right thing before waving to the officer standing nearby. Greg went behind the yellow line while Avery followed the walkway around the side of the house.

Savannah was leaning against the brick, one hand pressed to her stomach. The other held a small, white dog. Avery rushed to her sister's side. "Are you okay?"

"Just nauseous." Savannah's chin trembled and she swallowed hard. "Rachel's dog was running around the yard and the back door was open, just like the neighbor said. I overheard Grady say...it looks like the scene at Marianne Jenkins's house."

She squeezed Savannah's arm. Avery had never met Rachel, but she knew her sister and the other woman were close. They worked together at the crisis center. "Is Rachel single?"

"Yes. Divorced actually. It became final last year. That's why the neighbor called me. Rachel told him months ago that I was her emergency contact. Her parents are both dead, and she doesn't have children."

"Does she have any connection to Harrison University?"

Savannah nodded, tears welling in her eyes.

"She's attending part-time. She's one semester away from completing her bachelor's degree."

Avery bit the inside of her cheek to keep from crying. Her sister's grief was heartbreaking. "I'll have an officer take you home."

"No. Not yet." Savannah closed her eyes and leaned her head against the brick. "I'll be fine. I just need a moment. Go do your job, Avery."

She wanted to argue with her sister, but that would only waste time. Instead, she squeezed Savannah's arm once more before approaching the back door. It was splintered at the lock. Someone had pried it open.

Troopers were in the kitchen. One of them directed her to the back of the house. Avery walked through the living room on hollow legs. She took a deep breath, settling her emotions, before crossing the threshold into the master bedroom. Bedsheets were tangled and hanging from the bed. Items from the nightstand—a cell phone, a lamp, and a romance book—were scattered across the carpet. Grady and Weston turned as she entered, their conversation abruptly ending. Both men wore grim expressions.

"He attacked her while she was sleeping," Avery said. "That's consistent with Marianne Jenkins."

"Yes," Grady said. His jaw tightened. "It appears she was taken sometime earlier this evening. The neighbor spotted the back door open an hour ago and called it in."

Avery's chest tightened. Photographs lined the top of the dresser. She moved closer and Weston joined her. He pointed to a pretty dark-haired woman with a wide smile and a high forehead. "That's Rachel."

"The picture was taken during her first international trip last year," Savannah said from the doorway. The color had returned to her face. "She went to Spain. It was one of her life-long dreams—"

Avery's cell phone rang, cutting Savannah off. She fished it from her back pocket. The number was blocked. "Hello."

"Avery, we finally get the chance to speak. I've waited so long."

A cold shiver ran down her spine. The caller was using a voice distorter, but the words were still clear. She waved a hand to hush everyone in the room and put the call on speaker. "Who is this?"

"You know exactly who this is. Normally I would never talk during a chess game, but we're in between moves, so it's permissible." He paused. "Watching my television is very enlightening. I see from the news you've figured out Rachel is missing."

Her heart leapt into her throat and a sick feeling twisted her stomach. Grady was already whispering to someone on his cell phone, no doubt attempting to trace the call. Weston used his own phone to record the conversation and waved his finger in a circular motion to indicate she should keep talking.

"What do you want?" she asked.

"Ahhh, that is the question, isn't it? Poor Avery. Must be hard for you. Not knowing why you've been selected to play the game with me."

She kept her tone conversational. "Enlighten me then."

"It's simple," he said. "Your father and mine were adversaries. Their battle ended in a shootout, and your father killed mine. I want a rematch."

Avery mind raced. Was he talking about Jack Starin? Had to be. Her father had only used deadly force once during his career. But they'd done a search on Jack and hadn't uncovered any children. "What's your father's name?"

"Tsk, tsk, Avery. You don't expect me to do all the work for you. I've given you a clue to run down. I'm sure you can take it from there."

She sensed he was about to hang up. Panic set in. Had Grady managed to trace the call? *Think, think.*

"How do I know you're the Chessmaster?" Avery asked, stalling.

"I thought you might ask for proof," he said.

The distorted voice was creepy. "Rachel, dear, give a shout so Avery knows it's you."

A woman's terrified scream came over the line, distinct and clear since the voice distorter had been switched off. The woman muttered some incoherent words before screaming again. It iced Avery's blood. "Stop! Stop hurting her."

The scream cut off. Savannah swayed, her face pale, and Weston wrapped his arm around her waist to hold her up. Avery met her sister's eyes. Savannah nodded, her expression stark, answering Avery's silent question. The woman was Rachel.

"Do you see me now, Avery?" the Chessmaster whispered. "Do you understand?"

She shook, her hand gripping the phone so tightly it was a wonder she didn't snap the thing in two. "If you want me, then come and get me. Let Rachel go. This is between us."

He let out a breath that whispered over the line. "Soon, Avery. Very soon."

FIFTEEN

Rain pattered against the window in Avery's office, as she escorted Greg Kilbourne to the door. The interview had eaten an hour of her time, and she was anxious to have it over with. Her entire morning had been spent dealing with the dean, arranging for the open house, and talking to reporters. The rangers were tackling the murders, but every minute in the search for Rachel counted.

Avery opened her office door. "The dean is expecting you in his office. I can have an officer escort you."

"No need." Greg smirked. "I know the way. You have your hands full between the murders and the open house kicking off this afternoon."

Avery had delegated security of the open house to her deputy chief. He was capable of handling the event, although it left her short-handed in the murder investigation. Frustration nipped at her, and she had the sense Greg knew it.

Weston came out of the break room and joined them. Greg shook his hand before heading to the front of the station.

"Something about that guy bugs me," Avery muttered, once Greg was out of earshot.

"Me too." Weston rocked on his heels. "Some reporters have a sense of conscience, but I get the impression Greg isn't one of them."

"No, he isn't." She went back into her office. Weston followed, and she shut the door behind him. "But Greg's agreed to hold back the notes, along with the handmade bracelets each woman was wearing. In exchange, I agreed to admit the two murders and this recent abduction are related. He's going to run a full-page spread and give interviews with local news stations. I pray the increased attention will yield some new leads."

"Every little bit helps," Weston said, setting the file folder on her desk. "The crime scene investigators searched Rachel's house and came up empty-handed. No prints and no DNA. We've canvassed the neighborhood, but none of the neighbors saw anything suspicious. According to Rachel's friends and coworkers, she never complained of anyone watching her or expressed concerns about her safety."

So, they had nothing. The weight of it pressed down on Avery. She sank into her chair and yanked open her desk drawer. She rummaged around until she found her secret stash of chocolate peanut butter cups. "I'm really hoping you have some good news in that folder of yours."

He chuckled. "How about mixed news?"

"Better than nothing." She tossed him a

chocolate and opened one for herself. "Hit me with it."

"We located some cousins of Jack Starin. Turns out he did have a son. Nolan Starin."

Her heart skipped a beat. Weston pulled out a mug shot and pushed it across the desk toward her. The man staring back at her was hardened by time and middle age. Gray streaked his dark hair at the temples and he had a nasty scar along his chin. The information under the photo was from three years ago. It listed Nolan as a forty-five-year-old white male, 6'2", with brown eyes.

"Why didn't we find Nolan during our initial search?" Avery asked.

"Because Jack was a teenager when Nolan was born. Nolan's mother died in childbirth, and he was adopted and raised by his maternal grandparents. They lived in Houston, but according to the extended family, Nolan would travel to Union County often to visit his father. Unfortunately, the grandparents are both deceased." Weston sighed. "And, it seems, Nolan may be too."

Avery blinked, certain she'd misheard him. "I'm sorry. Excuse me?"

"Nolan was sentence to a long stint in prison —twenty years, in fact—after he kidnapped and assaulted a college student. With credit for good behavior, he got out early and was placed on parole. Six months later, he failed to show up for a meeting with his parole officer. Police were sent to his address. They found a huge amount of blood in the kitchen and evidence of a struggle."

"But no body?"

"No. They classified it as missing, presumed dead. According to the detective I spoke to, it was impossible for Nolan to have survived." He held up a finger in anticipation of her next question. "They did a DNA test and confirmed the blood was Nolan's."

She bit into her chocolate and chewed furiously. "When did this happen?"

"Three years ago." Weston tossed his

wrapper in the trash. "The extended family I spoke to haven't heard from Nolan since."

"Seems awfully convenient." Whoever was committing these murders was smart and understood police procedure. The Chessmaster was capable of faking his own death. "What do we know about the kidnapping and assault Nolan was convicted of?"

"He stalked and terrorized a college student for almost a year before he broke into her home and attacked her. Nolan attempted to strangle her with a rope, but her roommate came home early from work because she was sick, and the two women were able to escape."

"Sounds similar to the assault Nolan's dad, Jack, committed."

Weston nodded. "About that. We finally located Beverly Wilkins's case file. It makes for interesting reading. Your friend Calvin was right. The sheriff's department covered up Mike's incident with the patrol car. The case file reports the evidence was stolen but doesn't say how. Your dad, Kenneth, never let up on the case."

"That's not surprising." She tossed her own candy wrapper in the trash. "My dad was as stubborn as I am."

Weston briefly smiled before his expression grew serious again. "Jack Starin learned the evidence from the assault had been stolen. He started stalking and terrorizing his victim, Beverly. Kenneth worked hard to protect her, but the stalking laws twenty years ago were nonexistent. He pulled Jack in for questioning but got nowhere. Kenneth followed Jack, trying to catch him in violation of the law, anything he could do to keep the man in jail and away from Beverly."

"The Chessmaster mentioned last night that his father and mine had battled it out. That's what he was talking about."

"Yes. Jack broke into Beverly's home, cutting himself in the process. He left fingerprints and blood behind. It was the break your dad needed. When Kenneth showed up to arrest him, Jack opened fire. Your dad's life was threatened. He returned fire and Jack was killed."

Avery let out a breath. "And now Nolan wants revenge. What was the word he used? A rematch."

"Or someone wants us to think he does."

She reared back. "What do mean?"

He was quiet for a long moment. "It would be easy for Mike Steel to point us in this direction. He had access to all of the files and could've kept tabs on Nolan."

She let out a long breath. Weston was right. "Has anyone questioned Mike about where he was last night?"

"His lawyer refuses to allow any questioning. He also won't consent to a search of Mike's house, and we don't have enough evidence to get a warrant. I got permission for undercover officers to watch Mike after our initial conversation with him yesterday, but they arrived after Rachel went missing."

She rose from her chair and walked over to

the window behind her desk. Beyond the glass, people rushed by on the sidewalk. Their umbrellas fluttered in the wind. She wanted to protect every female on campus but felt powerless to do so.

Lord, every step forward is another step back. Please, help me.

Weston came up next to her. He didn't try to make her feel better with false pretenses. Instead, he was quiet, his broad shoulders squared, his mouth firmly set. It was something she was coming to rely on. His strength and partnership. The knowledge that every frustration she had about this case, he shared. And it made her feel less lonely at a time where guilt and worry might've eaten her alive.

Avery took a deep breath. "Okay, so there are two strong options. One possibility is that Nolan faked his own death and has come back to Union County in some twisted effort to get revenge for his father's death. The second possibility is that the murders are being committed by Mike, who's pretending to be Nolan, hoping we'll spend our time chasing a dead man."

"That sums it up. Grady and Luke are re-working the two murders from scratch, along with Rachel's abduction. They're looking for a connection to Mike or anything that would lead to a new suspect."

"Then you and I should stay with Nolan. Let's assume he faked his own death." Avery took a step backward and leaned against her desk. "If Nolan wanted to move back to Union County and not be recognized, he'd have plastic surgery to change his appearance. He'd obtain a fake ID. Essentially, he'd wipe the slate clean."

Weston nodded. "With the right surgeon, he could look completely different. Nolan could be anyone."

"Does he have the funds for that?"

"He does. Nolan inherited a lot of money from his maternal grandparents. According to the family members I spoke to, the money was moved to an offshore account."

They really were chasing a ghost. Avery rubbed her forehead. "What do we know about Nolan's activities here in Union County?"

"Not much. After Jack died, Nolan never came back. However, he was arrested a few times here in his twenties."

"What for?"

Weston reached around her and pulled over his file folder. "Once for drugs. A couple of times for petty theft. He never served jail time."

"Anyone get arrested with him?"

Weston frowned. "Yeah, one guy. Tom Belvin. I was about to run him through the system—"

She shot to her feet. "No need. I know who he is. Tom Belvin is the mailman we talked to outside of Debra's house. What were Nolan and Tom arrested for?"

"That was the drug charge. Officer pulled them over for a traffic stop and found marijuana in the car."

Her mind raced, different possibilities

pulling at her attention. "Who was the arresting officer?"

Weston flipped the page. His mouth tightened. "Mike Steel."

***

Weston followed Avery through the Union County Post Office to the sorting room. His boots tapped against the sealed concrete floor. The building was chilly, and the postal worker leading them to Tom Belvin wore fingerless gloves.

"Hey, Tom." She knocked on the open doorway frame. "You've got visitors." The worker turned to Weston and whispered, "I'll make sure no one comes back here for the next fifteen minutes."

"Appreciate it." He gave a sharp nod before stepping into the room.

It was windowless, the fluorescent lights overhead creating harsh brights and shadows. Tom paused, his hand hovering over a bucket of

RANGER COURAGE

mail. It appeared he was sorting his portion for delivery.

"Hi, Avery." Tom's brow crinkled. "And... Weston, right?"

"Good memory." Weston smiled, attempting to put the other man at ease. "Sorry to interrupt you while you're working, but there have been developments in Debra's case. We wanted to talk to you again."

"I heard about her boyfriend Victor Haas on the news." Tom placed some letters into the carton. "If you're looking for additional information about him, I can't tell you anything more."

"We need to ask about someone else. Nolan Starin."

Tom froze before slowly turning to face them. "Isn't he dead?"

Weston studied the other man. There was something in the curve of his mouth and the furrow of his brow. Forced surprise, maybe? Tom's reaction didn't come off as genuine.

"Technically, he's classified as missing."

Weston left out the presumed-dead part. He wanted to gauge how much Tom knew. "When's the last time you saw or spoke to Nolan?"

His gaze darted to Avery before focusing back on Weston. "Uhhh, musta been close to twenty years now."

"Then why did you think he was dead?"

"My mom. She's a news junky and all over social media. She read about it or something and mentioned it to me. But I swear, Mom told me Nolan was dead. Why are you asking about him?" He stiffened. "Is this connected to the murders? Another woman was taken this morning, right? I saw it on TV."

Avery showed him a photograph of Rachel Long. "Do you know her?"

Tom fiddled with a button on his uniform as his gaze dropped to the picture. "Yeah, that's Rachel. She works at the crisis center. When I deliver certified letters, sometimes she'll sign for them."

A knot formed in Weston's stomach. Tom

admitted knowing Debra Channing and now Rachel Long. He'd been friends with Nolan twenty years ago. That gave him person-of-interest status. Maybe he was the one pinning these murders on Nolan.

"You mentioned the last time you saw or spoke to Nolan was twenty years ago," Weston said, keeping his tone casual. "That was around the time his father, Jack Starin, died."

Tom grabbed some more letters and tossed them in the bucket without looking at them. "Yeah."

"Were you and Nolan good friends?"

"Nolan didn't have friends." Tom's mouth hardened. "He was a bully and a creep. When he left town, it was a blessing."

"Why is that?" Weston asked.

Tom's hand tightened on the mail bucket. "Because Nolan was one scary guy. Even back then when we were young. His dad, well, you know what *he* did. Attacking a woman and nearly killing her. What's that old saying? The apple doesn't fall far from the tree. That was Nolan. He was a killer in training."

Avery tilted her head. "If Nolan was so terrifying, why did you hang out with him?"

Tom's shoulders sagged, and he scrubbed a hand through his thinning blond hair. "My parents were good people, but I got mixed up in the wrong crowd in high school. Nolan didn't live in Union County, but he spent the summers here. He was incredibly smart and excellent at manipulating people." He drew in a breath. "Nolan wanted me to steal from my parents. I refused. The next day, my dog...my dog was nailed to a tree in my backyard. He'd been torn apart. Nolan did it to teach me a lesson. Once you were in his web, it was impossible to get out."

"Why didn't you report him to the police?" Avery asked.

"Because the police wouldn't have been able to protect me or my family, and Nolan would only do something worse. Instead, I did what he said and didn't ask questions."

There was a raw thread of fear running through Tom's voice. Weston wasn't immune to it. He softened his stance. "How did Nolan react when his dad died?"

"He was furious and talked about getting revenge." Tom glanced at Avery, and a pained look came over his face. "Every scenario involved your dad."

"Except Nolan never acted on his threats," Avery said. "Why do you think that is?"

"Honestly, Nolan was scared of your dad. Don't get me wrong, Nolan was dangerous. But he was only twenty and had a healthy fear of prison. His dad, Jack, told him horror stories about jail and swore he'd never go back."

Weston was getting mixed signals from Tom. In one breath, he was terrified of Nolan; in the next, he shared family stories. "Did you spend a lot of time with Nolan and his dad?"

Tom shrugged. "Enough. Like I said, I was young and stupid."

Yeah, definitely mixed signals. Why would Tom hang out with Nolan if he was terrified of him? Victim and abuser could sometimes be a complicated relationship, and it sounded like Nolan was emotionally and mentally abusing Tom. The dog story demonstrated that. Still, something was off.

"What else can you tell us about Jack?" he asked.

"Well, Jack took pleasure in taunting the police. Jack and Nolan used to strategize on the next move. They both thought they were smarter than the cops." Tom rocked back on his heels. "I'm happy to say they were wrong."

Avery frowned. "Hold on, so you knew Jack had assaulted Beverly and you never went to the police?"

She tried to hide her disgust, but Weston heard the vibration of it in her voice. He shared her feelings.

Tom glared at her. "Didn't you hear me say earlier that Nolan killed my dog? Nolan worshipped his father. If I went to the police and reported Jack, Nolan would've killed me. No question." He grabbed the bucket of mail and lifted it off the counter. "Now, I really need to go. I'm late."

He pushed past them, and this time, Weston let him. Tom paused in the doorway. "Do you really think Nolan could be back in town, murdering women?"

"Is he capable of faking his own death and creating a new identity?" Avery asked. "Smart enough to evade the police? Cruel enough to kill?"

Tom took a shaky breath. "The answer to all of that is yes. And if Nolan is behind this, then Avery, you should be careful. He didn't get revenge on your dad, but Nolan's older now. I wouldn't put it past him to try his hand with you."

SIXTEEN

Weston chugged his fifth cup of coffee and studied the whiteboard. It was Friday evening. Rachel had been missing for nineteen hours, and they were no closer to finding her.

Beside him, Avery briefly touched her temple. Probably nursing another headache. Harrison University's open house was underway, and while Avery had delegated much of the work for the event, security issues had come up. Weston had done his best to help shoulder the burden, but it wasn't enough. There were shadows under Avery's eyes and her complexion was pale.

Grady, along with Emilia, walked into the conference room. Both looked as exhausted as Weston felt. Grady had the sleeves of his shirt rolled up and hadn't shaved since yesterday. Emilia's hair was pulled back into a messy bun. They carried takeaway coffee cups.

"Sorry to keep you waiting," Grady said. "Let's jump right in. We got a break in Rachel's case. A neighbor saw a delivery van on Rachel's street half an hour before she was taken. Considering the lateness of the hour, he wrote down the license plate."

Weston straightened. "And?"

"The plates were stolen from long-term parking at Austin-Bergstrom International Airport. We questioned Marianne's neighbors again. One remembered a delivery van on her street as well. A white van with Texas plates and a small company logo on the side. We traced the van from a gas station security camera. Different plates than the van on Rachel's street. Also stolen. The company logo had been changed."

"He's one step ahead of us," Avery said. "The logo is probably a stick on. He can switch them, along with plates."

Emilia nodded. "This is pretty detailed planning. I believe the killer has knowledge of law enforcement procedures. Additionally, Harrison University is a comfortable space for him, and so is Union County."

"What do you mean by comfortable?" Avery asked.

"Leaving Debra in the classroom and Marianne at your house was risky. The killer had to be familiar with both spaces, and confident enough to believe he wouldn't get caught. Either he grew up here or has lived in town for a while." Emilia swept a hand across her forehead, knocking the bangs out of her eyes. "We're looking for a white male, thirty to fifty. He has intimate knowledge about Jack Starin's death. The killer is intelligent, organized, and a chess fan."

Weston scanned the whiteboard and the photographs of the women. He pointed to Rachel. "What chess piece does she represent? Debra was a pawn and Marianne a rook. Is Rachel a knight?"

Emilia shook her head. "A knight is a soldier, so no. I think Rachel is a bishop. In medieval times, bishops were influential. Rachel worked at the crisis center, mostly doing fundraising. She's a people person and successful in getting donations."

"Let's look at our top three suspects using Emilia's profile," Grady said. "There's Nolan Starin. Missing and presumed dead, based on the evidence found in his apartment, including signs of a struggle and large amounts of blood. I've seen the DNA report and can confirm the blood is Nolan's. None of his cousins or old friends have heard from him since the day he went missing. There's no indication he's alive. Of course, that doesn't wipe him off the suspect list, but it's more likely the real killer is using Nolan as a scapegoat."

Avery's brow creased. "If Nolan faked his death for the specific purpose of enacting revenge, he'd avoid contacting his friends or family. He has a violent criminal history, including stalking and strangling women in a manner similar to our victims."

"Those are good points, Avery," Emilia said. "And normally I would argue Nolan should be our top suspect. Problem is, Nolan had years to come after you but didn't. What triggered him now?"

"My move home. I arrived in town six months ago. There were articles in the local newspaper announcing my position with Harrison University."

Grady frowned. "It'll be difficult to track individuals who moved to town six months ago, but we could take a pass at new students and faculty. If Nolan is using a fake ID, we might spot an inconsistency." He made a note on the whiteboard.

It was another thread to pull, and Weston was grateful. Police work was tedious, but every detail was important. One of them could crack the case wide open.

"Let's assume Nolan is dead," Weston said. "The killer has intimate knowledge of the events surrounding Jack Starin's death, along with Nolan's murder."

Grady tapped the marker against the whiteboard. "That brings us to our other two suspects, Mike Steel and Nolan's best friend, Tom Belvin. On the surface, Tom fits Emilia's profile. Thirty-seven, college educated, well-liked, born and raised in Union County. He admitted knowing two of the victims. One arrest for drug possession years ago, otherwise, Tom's criminal record is clean. After interviewing friends and coworkers—including a couple of ex-girlfriends —there's no indication he's violent."

"So we can't eliminate him," Avery said. "But he's not a top suspect."

"Correct," Grady said. "Which brings us to Detective Mike Steel. He fits Emilia's profile perfectly, down to being a chess champion. He doesn't have an alibi for any of the abductions.

Mike applied for the university's Chief of Police position. He was interviewed several times, but when asked about his previous history with alcohol, Mike got defensive. The dean felt Mike failed to recognize his own mistakes, and told him so."

Avery's mouth flattened. "And then they hired me."

There was a faint hint of vulnerability in her tone and Weston stepped closer, as if he could shield her from the pain. He hated to see Avery hurting.

"That may have been the trigger," Emilia said. "From Mike's point of view, his career was destroyed by your dad, and then he lost a valuable position to you. He decides to get revenge. His primary target is you, Avery, but by killing women associated with Harrison University, he also damages the school."

Weston rocked back on his heels. Everything lined up. "Has Mike been questioned again?"

"We've tried several times." Grady

frowned. "His attorney keeps shooting us down. The sheriff allowed us to search Mike's desk and locker, but it didn't yield any new leads or establish a connection between Mike and the women."

"Have you traced the killer's phone call to Avery?" Weston asked.

Grady hooked a thumb in his belt. "The killer is tech savvy. He used a burner phone to call Avery, and then turned it off. We can't get a location. I have technicians keeping an eye on it, but unless the killer uses the phone again, we won't pin him down."

"Well, that doesn't sound like Mike," Avery said. "When the sheriff's department switched to tablets for reports, it took Mike months to figure the system out. He complained about it constantly."

Weston shrugged. "He could've been faking."

"Maybe, but what if we're focused on the wrong suspect?" Avery asked. "I have trouble believing Mike snapped and suddenly started killing women to get back at me and my dad over a job."

"Avery..." Weston shifted in his boots, trying to figure out the best way to say her perspective was compromised due to her personal relationship with Mike.

Avery blushed and her shoulders turned inward. "I know how it sounds. I get it."

Emilia's gaze locked on Avery's face. "But you think we're missing something?"

"I don't know. Mike's reaction when we confronted him was off. He was furious. Insulted, really. If he was the Chessmaster, wouldn't he have planned his answers better? We could be barking up the wrong tree and end up missing the killer in the process."

Weston studied the whiteboard. Avery was right. They didn't have a shred of hard evidence linking Mike to these murders. It was all suspicion and supposition. Emilia's profile was an important tool, but it wasn't proof.

"No one wants to overlook anything,"

Grady said. "Trust me. We're tracking down every lead. We just don't have much to go on."

"Meanwhile Rachel is still missing." Avery ran a hand through her hair. "I released a statement asking for information about Nolan Starin to the media. The crisis center is running a tip line, and volunteers are spreading flyers around town. I'd like to check in with them. Maybe there's a new lead."

Weston glanced at Grady. There was worry in his fellow ranger's expression, concern Weston shared. Was Avery right? Were they narrowing in on the wrong man?

Avery spent the car ride second-guessing herself. When Weston put the truck in Park at the crisis center, she undid her seatbelt. "You think I'm wrong about Mike, don't you?"

He hesitated. "Honestly, I don't know. You have insight into Mike I don't. You know him well. At the same time—"

"I could be in denial because he's my friend."

"Yes."

Weston confirmed her own suspicions. Her emotions were muddled by a combination of exhaustion and worry. Where was Rachel now? Was the Chessmaster hurting her? The echo of Rachel's screams kept playing in Avery's head over and over.

She exited the truck and shivered against the rush of cold air. Weston came around the vehicle and hugged her. Some of the tension in her shoulders eased away. His jacket was soft under her cheek, and she could make out the faint beat of his heart.

Avery lifted her face, and Weston kissed her. It was soft and gentle and filled with the promise of more. Avery's breath hitched. "What was that for?"

The corner of his mouth lifted. "I needed it. Do you mind?"

"No." She rose on her tiptoes and kissed him again. Ill-advised, perhaps, because every touch between them cracked the walls around her heart even more.

She dropped back to her heels, and Weston brushed the hair away from her face. His touch sent heat straight through her, and the look in his eyes yanked on her heart. Buried in those brown depths was a wealth of emotion.

This was hard for him. A killer was stalking and threatening her, and Weston had lost the last woman he loved. Not to violence, but Melissa had died all the same. Yet he didn't pull away or deny his feelings. Instead, he stepped forward. Weston had treated her with honesty, kindness, and consideration. She tightened her arms around his waist.

Avery had made a terrible mistake with her ex-fiancé, Jeffrey. She'd ignored her own instincts, the soft whisper inside her heart, indicating something was wrong. She'd stuck with him—in part because she genuinely cared—but also because she used logic to make her decisions instead of her heart.

What was that phrase? God speaks in the

silence of the heart. Well, she hadn't listened. Not when it came to her relationship with Jeffery.

Things with Weston were complicated, and the timing was terrible. Avery didn't know what the future held. Weston might not be healed enough to fall in love again. Yet there was a tug in her heart, urging her forward in spite of her fears.

She would not make the same mistake twice. She would not ignore it.

Lord, I don't know where you are leading me, but I will follow. Guide me in the right direction.

Weston sighed, brushing his lips across the top of her head. "As much as I'd love to stay out here pretending the rest of the world doesn't exist..."

She stole one more kiss before backing out of his arms. "We have work to do. Come on."

They crossed the parking lot. A bell jingled as they entered the crisis center. Phones rang and volunteers answered them and took messages. Flyers containing Rachel Long's photograph along with information about her abduction were scattered around the room. Avery knew hundreds more were plastered across town.

Savannah was behind the front desk. Her sister looked exhausted but moved with practiced efficiency. When she caught sight of Avery, a mixture of hope and fear crossed her features.

"Nothing yet," Avery said. "Has anyone come forward with new information?"

Savannah shook her head. "I've been coordinating with Luke, and all leads are being followed up on, but nothing concrete."

A familiar voice called Avery's name, and she turned. Nana waved from the back of the room. She was standing with Calvin. The retired FBI agent had traded his waders for soft slacks and a button-down flannel shirt. He'd arrived after news about Rachel Long's disappearance broke and was assisting with the tip line.

Calvin was talking to an older woman with dyed black hair and an expensive purse. Avery immediately recognized her as Marigold Sampson. Her husband had been the pastor of their church when she was growing up.

"Avery, dear, you have perfect timing," Nana said. "Marigold has information about the case."

Avery's heart skipped a beat. "Regarding?"

"Nolan Starin." Marigold shifted in her black flats, and color rose in her cheeks. "Forgive me if I'm overstepping, but I heard on the news you're looking for information about him and his family."

"We are," Avery said. "Nana and Calvin, would you give us a few minutes with Mrs. Sampson please?"

"Of course." Nana stepped over to a closed door. "Why don't you use Savannah's office? I'm sure she won't mind."

There were only two chairs inside the office, so Avery gestured for Marigold to take one while she sat in the other. Weston remained standing, but his posture was relaxed. Marigold's gaze darted in his direction, and Avery belatedly realized she'd never introduced them. "Oh, I'm sorry. Mrs. Sampson, this is Texas Ranger Weston Donovan. He's working with me on the case."

"Pleasure to meet you, ma'am." Weston shook her hand and gave her a reassuring smile, flashing his dimples. "Appreciate you coming in."

Marigold was over eighty-five, but even she wasn't immune to the ranger's charm. She blushed and smiled back. "Glad to help. Now I don't want either of you to think I'm gossiping."

"We won't," Avery said. "What can you tell us about Nolan?"

"Well, he came from a troubled family. Nolan worshipped his father, but Jack Starin was a complicated man. Abusive to his wife, yet charming to neighbors and friends."

Avery nodded. Manipulative. That sounded familiar. Marigold's comments echoed Tom Belvin's.

Marigold set her purse on her lap. "Jack was smart, and he passed those brains on to Nolan, along with a good dose of sneakiness. Now Nolan didn't live with his dad full-time. He was raised by his maternal grandparents. But every summer when he came to town, Nolan started problems and involved the local kids in his troublemaking."

"Mrs. Sampson, it's our understanding Nolan and Tom Belvin were friends," Weston said. "How close were they?"

"Very close. It didn't start out that way, a'-course. But after Nolan and Tom found out they were half-brothers everything changed."

Avery sat up straighter. "I'm sorry. Hold on. Did you say Tom Belvin is Nolan's half-brother?"

Marigold blinked. "Yes, dear. Tom's mother had an affair with Jack Starin. There was trouble in Mrs. Belvin's marriage, as can happen from time to time. After the affair ended, the Belvins came to my husband for spiritual advice. They decided to stay together and raise Tom. Jack left them alone for a bit, but when Tom turned, well, I dunno, twelve or thirteen, Jack told him the truth."

"Tom lied to us," she whispered. "Everything we thought about Nolan applies to Tom." Avery shot from the chair. "I'm sorry, Mrs. Sampson, we need to go."

Weston opened the door, his cell phone to his ear, already snapping out orders. They hightailed to the exit and raced across the parking lot. Avery sent up a prayer as Weston peeled onto the street, lights flashing and siren blaring.

Rachel, hold on. We're coming.

SEVENTEEN

Avery gripped the handle above the truck's door as Weston took a sharp right turn. She glanced at the GPS and pointed down the block. "There. That's Tom's house."

Her heart jumped. Flames were shooting out of the house at the end of the street. "Tom's house is on fire."

Neighbors were gathered in the street. Smoke wisped in the air, although the front of the home appeared undamaged. Avery undid her seat belt and radioed in the information. Backup was five minutes out. Weston pulled to a stop.

A bald man ran toward her as Avery hopped out of the truck. He was holding a cell phone. "You guys were fast. I just called 911."

"Is anyone in the home?" Avery asked.

"Tom's SUV is gone, so I don't think he's inside, but I can't say for sure. I live next door and heard the smoke detector going off."

"Okay, we need you and the rest of the neighbors to stay back and keep the street clear for the fire trucks."

She sprinted across the yard and joined Weston, who was already on the front porch. He knocked on the door and announced himself as a police officer before trying the handle. A search warrant wasn't needed since the house was on fire. They had a duty to verify no one was inside, possibly hurt.

The knob twisted open.

"Convenient," Avery muttered under her breath, pulling her weapon. Union County was a small town, but people didn't often leave their front doors unlocked. Especially when they weren't home. She clicked on her flashlight.

Weston eased the door open with his foot. "Tom, it's the police. Are you here?"

Avery's heart pounded in tune to the wailing smoke detector. Announcing themselves was dangerous. This could be a trap. Still, they didn't have hard evidence Tom was the Chessmaster. He was a liar, sure, but that didn't make him a killer.

A momentary sense of panic jittered through Avery as she stepped into the dark living room. She shone her light around the space, checking for Tom. Not here. She followed Weston as he moved into the dining room. The smoke cast a hazy fog over everything. Duty kept her feet moving forward. Tom could be injured and unable to escape. The acrid scent of soot burned her lungs.

"Tom," she yelled over the screaming smoke detector. "Police. Can you hear me?"

No response. Weston pointed to the kitchen, and Avery nodded. The smoke grew thicker. A gas stove hunched in the corner, flames shooting from one of its burners. A charred dish towel rested on the burner next to a boiling pot of water.

Avery flicked off the burner and poured water from the faucet to douse the flames. It hissed and popped against the overheated metal stove. Had Tom gotten burned or hurt while cooking? Or had the fire been set to lure police to his house?

She pressed on Weston's back to indicate he should move forward, and together they followed the hallway to the back bedrooms. A light from the room on the end poured across the carpet.

"Police," Weston called out. "Tom, are you here? Do you need help?"

Avery swiveled into the closest room. Packing boxes lined the wall, next to a rack of clothes. She quickly cleared the attached bathroom and closet. Empty.

She rejoined Weston in the hall. He stood in the doorway of the lit bedroom. Something in his posture, in the twist of his shoulders made her heart pick up speed. Rachel? She closed the distance between them.

He held out a hand. "It's not her, Avery." His expression was stark. "Neither Rachel nor Tom is here, and I don't think—"

She pushed past him into the room and then drew up short. The blood drained to her feet, lightheadedness combined with adrenaline narrowed her vision. She couldn't breathe. Couldn't move.

A female mannequin, dressed in a police uniform and wearing a wig of copper-colored hair, hung from a noose. Smoke curled around the room, casting an eerie fog. The doll's facial features were strikingly similar to Avery's own, and somewhere in the back part of her mind, she wondered if it'd been specially made. She clung to the thought. Held on with the fierce knowledge that she was on the verge of passing out and needed something—anything—to stop the quaking of her body.

Weston came in front of her, dipping his

head to catch her gaze. "I won't let him touch you, Avery. It's not going to happen." He placed a hand on her bicep, the heat of his palm sinking straight through the sleeve of her uniform. "I'll die first."

She let out the breath she was holding, tears pricking her eyes. "Don't you get it, Weston? That's exactly what I'm afraid of. How many more people will die?"

Within an hour, Tom's house was swarming with crime scene investigators. Weston stepped out of the kitchen. Avery was leaning against a pillar on the back porch, one arm wrapped around her midsection. In the other hand, she held a takeaway cup. She spotted him and extended it out. "Want some coffee? A patrol officer was kind enough to bring me one."

Weston wanted to tuck Avery in a faraway place where she would be safe. But that wasn't going to happen. She was a cop, first and foremost. Avery would never abandon her duty or the people counting on her. He took the coffee cup and glared over the crime scene. "Which officer?"

"Why are you asking?"

"So I can tell him to stop making the moves on you. Bringing coffee is a telltale sign of interest." He took a sip of the fragrant brew. "Oh, yeah and he splurged for extra hazelnut cream. Definitely need to have a talk with him."

She laughed, and a sweet blush crept across her cheeks. "Stand down, Ranger. He's twenty-five if he's a day. Too young for my taste."

Weston leaned against the railing next to her. "Really? What is your type?"

Her blush deepened, and Weston drank it in. It was far better than the stark fear that had been in her eyes an hour ago. Avery's words had been ringing in his head on repeat.

That's exactly what I'm afraid of. How many more people will die?

Her concern for the victims—including potential ones, like Weston—didn't surprise him.

Spending every day and night together had given him a crash course in Avery. She was a nurturer, and the killer was zeroing in on her Achilles' heel.

As if she were reading Weston's thoughts, the smile melted from Avery's face. She glanced at the back door and the investigators inside. "I hate this."

"We all hate it." He elbowed her gently. "You're not in this alone."

"I know, but he's going after these people because of me. To torture and hurt me. It's..."

"Sick and demented." He pinned her with a look. "And not your fault."

"Doesn't feel that way."

"Do you blame your dad? The Chess-master is aiming for you, because of actions your dad took."

"My dad didn't do anything—" Her gaze narrowed. "I see where you're going with this."

"Good." He stole another sip of her coffee, wincing at the sugary sweetness. "And next time you order coffee, can you make it black? This stuff is awful."

She swiped the cup back. "No one is forcing you to drink it."

The backyard gate clanged shut. Luke came around the side of the house seconds later. His expression was thunderous. "Mike Steel is missing."

"How?" Weston stood. "He was being watched by undercover officers."

"Apparently, he hasn't been home since Rachel went missing. His lawyer claims Mike isn't under arrest and is free to leave town. He refuses to disclose his client's location. I'm getting a court order to compel him to tell us, but honestly, I suspect he doesn't know."

"So we can't eliminate Mike as a suspect," Avery said. "And things with Tom are as clear as mud."

"Fill me in," Luke said.

Weston hooked his thumbs on his pockets. "Tom's computers are locked down with a security password, so it's taking time to get into them. We have a BOLO out on his SUV. There's no sign of Rachel anywhere in the house, although the techs are still fingerprinting. We've also confirmed Nolan and Tom are half-brothers."

"How?"

"Tom's mom. Additionally, Tom visited Nolan in prison and listed himself as a brother in their records. He was Nolan's emergency contact."

Luke rocked back on his heels. "So we can't eliminate anyone as a suspect. Nolan, Tom, or Mike could be behind this."

"I—" Avery's phone rang. She glanced at the number and paled. "It's blocked."

The Chessmaster. Weston pulled out his own cell and started recording. "Answer it, Avery."

She squared her shoulders and hit the button flashing on the screen. "Hello."

"Congratulations, Avery." The man used a voice distorter, as he had during the previous phone call. "You saved my brother's house before it burned to the ground. He'll be happy."

"I want to speak with Tom," Avery said.

"He's indisposed at the moment."

Weston's gaze narrowed. The killer was playing with them. Tom could be the Chessmaster, or he could be one of his victims. They had no way of knowing for sure.

"Where is Rachel?" she asked.

The Chessmaster laughed.

The killer actually laughed. Weston gripped his cell phone harder and took a deep breath to keep his emotions in check. This man was never going to see the outside of a jail cell. He would make sure of it.

"Right to the point, aren't you, Avery? As a matter of fact, Rachel is the reason I'm calling. I've been thinking about what you said during our last phone call. You're right. It's not fair to remove your chess pieces without providing an opportunity to get one back."

Chess pieces. The man was talking about people, not that he cared. But the words chewed through Weston's gut with their coldness.

"So I would like to propose a trade," he continued. "You for Rachel."

Weston's breath lodged in his chest. He wouldn't let the killer anywhere near Avery.

Not on his watch. Not ever.

Avery arched her brows. "I want a guarantee you won't hurt Rachel. And I want proof she's alive."

"It's already done. Tell Ranger Donovan to check his email."

Weston quickly scrolled to the right app on his phone. Indeed there was a new email, sent moments ago. The sender was listed as the Chessmaster. He opened it, every heartbeat thundering in his ears. Rachel's wide eyes stared back at him from the screen. Terror was etched across her features. She was sitting in a dark room next to a television tuned to a local news channel broadcasting live from Tom's house.

Avery lifted her own phone closer to her

mouth. A vein in her forehead throbbed. "When and where?"

"I'll call you tomorrow afternoon with further instructions."

———

Grass crunched under Weston's boots as he swept the perimeter of the Madison house with his flashlight. His nerves were on edge and he couldn't sleep. The team had spent hours developing a plan to ambush the Chessmaster during the trade for Rachel, but there were too many unknowns to make it foolproof.

His cell phone beeped with an incoming text message. After reading it, he circled to the front of the house.

Grady got out of his truck. "Thought you might want an update, not that it's a great one."

Weston's shoulders tightened. "We've still got nothing."

"Yep. We can't determine if Tom is the Chessmaster, or one of his victims. Tom left work around six. A neighbor saw an SUV like the one Tom drives in the neighborhood around six thirty, but she didn't notice who was behind the wheel. There weren't any fingerprints in the house other than Tom's."

"His cell phone?"

"Missing. We've tried pinging it, but it's been turned off. The last known location was the post office parking lot." Grady zipped his jacket closed. "The Chessmaster could've ambushed Tom as he left work. Incapacitated him, turned off his cell, and drove Tom's vehicle—with Tom inside—to his house. Staged the mannequin, started the fire, and booked it."

Weston raked a hand through his hair. "Or Tom turned his cell off when he left work, drove home, staged the scene, set the fire, and left."

Grady nodded. "I tried tracing the Chessmaster's phone call along with the email he sent you, but like I said before, this guy is tech savvy. We've got nothing so far. Investigators will keep working on it, but unless something breaks free—"

"Avery will go through with the trade." Weston's teeth clenched. "It's a trap. The killer understands police procedure. He'll be counting on us to protect her, but I guarantee he has a plan around it."

"Avery understands the risk. She accepts them." Grady paused, his tone softening. "I don't normally push into your business, Weston, but this time there's no choice. I know you have feelings for Avery. Are they going to cloud your judgment during this operation?"

Heat flared in Weston's cheeks as a mixture of embarrassment and pride wrestled for use of his tongue. He would never allow his personal feelings to interfere with his job. At least...not until today. Hadn't he acted like a caged bear at the strategy meeting? Who was he kidding? Grady was right to ask.

Weston took a deep breath. "I have feelings for Avery and I'm worried about using her as bait, but I can handle it."

Grady nodded. "We're going to keep her safe, Weston."

"I know we're going to do everything possible, but nothing is certain." Weston was gripped with the same terrorizing powerlessness as when Melissa's cancer became terminal. It clamped down on him, making every breath painful. "I care about her, Grady, and it's my own fault for getting in this deep. I knew better than to get involved with a cop. Avery walks into danger, not out of it."

"So do you."

"But..." Weston didn't know how to explain. The devastation of losing his wife was a heavy scar on his heart. The pain had dulled, but the mark lingered, a reminder of the cost when he fell in love. "There's too much risk."

"People die in car accidents. From heart attacks. Aneurysms. I don't think it's Avery's profession that's holding you back." Grady shoved his hands in his pockets and sighed. "Before she passed, Melissa told me to encourage you to date."

"You never said anything before."

"You weren't ready to hear it. But now, it's important you do. I know you loved Melissa and she loved you. But Weston, she wanted you to have a full and happy life. So does God." Grady turned to face him. "From my point of view, you haven't so much as looked at another woman since Melissa died. Until Avery. I don't believe that's an accident."

Deep inside, Weston didn't either. There was something about Avery that got under his skin and into his heart in a way no one else had.

"Love is a decision, Weston, just like faith." Grady clapped him on the back. "Choose wisely, my friend."

He nodded. Grady left, and Weston watched the ranger's taillights fade. The quiet stillness of the night settled around him. His fingers went to the chain around his neck. He freed the wedding rings from under his shirt, his thumb tracing the familiar orbs.

Weston lifted his gaze to the starlit sky. *Lord, I need help.*

EIGHTEEN

Avery paced her office, coffee mug in hand. She'd switched to water after her third cup of coffee, but nothing was taking the edge off her exhaustion. In theory, going home to sleep after the strategy meeting last night had been a good idea. In actuality, she'd tossed and turned. Her cell phone sat on her desk.

"We've got SWAT on standby and under-cover officers as well," Luke said. "Everyone is ready to mobilize when the Chessmaster calls. Technicians will outfit you with a camera and microphone."

She nodded and took a drink of water. "I suspect he'll arrange to meet somewhere on campus. Open house events are happening all day. The sheer number of people will make it difficult to trap him."

Luke shoved his hands in his pockets. "It's difficult to know what to expect. Debra Channing's funeral is this afternoon. That may be the meeting place."

"Nana's at the church with Savannah, setting up for the funeral, and there are news crews already out front. It'll be difficult for the Chessmaster to slip in with Rachel and escape without being noticed. Doesn't mean he won't try, but I think he's smarter than that."

He scowled. "Honestly, Avery, I don't like any of this. There are too many variables we can't account for."

She didn't know what to say. Avery wanted to get Rachel back, and she was willing to sacrifice herself to do it, but she didn't want anyone else hurt in the process. Her hand tightened on the coffee mug and she glanced at her cell phone.

Luke followed her gaze and stepped closer. "No one would blame you for backing out."

His tone was gentle and concern was threaded in it. She met his gaze. "I would never forgive myself if I didn't try."

He shook his head. "You proved my wife right yet again. Megan told me that's what you would say." Luke shrugged. "But I had to make sure."

"Thank you. I'm lucky to count you and Megan as my friends." She checked her watch. "Do you know where Weston is? He disappeared over an hour ago."

"I'm right here," Weston said from the doorway behind her.

Butterflies fluttered in Avery's stomach. She turned. Weston's expression was carefully blank and he carried a bag in one hand. Since the Chessmaster's phone call yesterday, Weston had been...she didn't quite know how to describe it. Not rude. No, he'd never be that.

Distant.

It was the only word that came to mind. Like there was a wall around him, preventing Avery from reaching him. It was a self-defense mechanism. Mentally, she knew that. But the loss of his support cut her, far more than she'd anticipated and so much deeper than if Weston was merely a boyfriend. It'd taken her most of the night to figure out why.

She was falling in love with him.

When it happened, Avery didn't know. Maybe it'd been lingering under the surface for days, but the fear of getting hurt kept her from facing the truth. But last night, lying in bed, thinking about what would happen today, there was no refuting it.

"Luke, can I have a moment alone with Avery?" Weston asked.

"Sure." The ranger pushed away from the table. "I'm going to check the microphone/camera setup. I'll be back in five minutes."

Weston shut the door to Avery's office. The

blinds along the other windows were closed, affording them privacy.

Avery set her mug on the desk. "What's in the bag?"

"Something for you." He pulled out a tactical knife. It was a fixed blade with a serrated spine and a drop-point blade. "I know you carry a pocket knife, but this one is stronger. Bigger."

Avery crossed the room. Every step made her more aware of Weston. The sharp curves of his face, the small nick on his chin where he'd cut himself shaving, the way his shirt molded over his chest. Those butterflies inside her stomach took flight. She wanted to step on her tiptoes and brush her mouth against his.

Instead, Avery took the knife and tested the grip. It was lightweight and fit her hand perfectly. The blade shimmered under the fluorescent light as she swiped it through the air. The balance was smooth. "It's fantastic."

He pulled out a black band from the bag. "This sheath goes around your waist, above the duty belt. It'll place the knife here." Weston reached around and his fingers brushed the small of her back. "The blade will be concealed under your shirt, but still accessible with your right hand."

He didn't say it, but she heard the words all the same. *Just in case.* Avery carried protection on her duty belt, but if the Chessmaster got close enough to completely disarm her, there was a chance he would miss the hidden knife.

Avery's chest squeezed tight and it hurt to breathe. The gift was beyond thoughtful. "Thank you, Weston."

"You're welcome."

She put the knife and sheath back inside the bag. It was something to keep her hands busy, while her mind struggled to find the right words to say. "Weston, I know you disagree with my decision, but if there's any way to bring Rachel home, I have to take it. No matter the risk to myself."

"I know." He sighed. "My attitude has been less than stellar since last night, and I'm sorry.

Honestly, if the roles were reversed, I'd make the same decision you are. It's our job."

Some of the weight lifted from her shoulders. She set the bag on her desk. "I can't blame you for being upset. None of this is easy."

"No, but I haven't approached it the right way either. Last night, I spent a lot of time praying and soul-searching. About me and you. About us."

He looped his fingers around a chain hanging from his neck and pulled it over his head. Something dangled from the necklace. It took Avery a moment to realize it was two gold rings. One was large enough for a man, the other made for a woman.

Wedding rings. Avery's gaze lifted to meet Weston's. She couldn't read his expression, and a small bite of panic took hold. Was he about to tell her they were done? Now?

"Weston, I—"

"Let me say this, please." He cupped her shoulder gently, still holding up the rings. "I've been wearing these since the day Melissa died.

I thought they were a reminder of my marriage and everything I'd lost. But I was wrong. I'm wearing them as a symbol of what's possible."

She searched his face. "I'm not sure I understand."

"It's not a fear of moving on that's holding me back, Avery. I was nervous about choosing the wrong person to do it with. Rushing into a relationship to fill the void in my life would dishonor the love Melissa showed me was attainable. That's why I'm wearing the rings. As a reminder to wait until the right person comes into my life." Weston traced his hand down her sleeve and lifted her hand. He dropped the rings in Avery's open palm and closed her fingers around them. "But I don't need to wear them anymore. Because I found you."

Her breath caught and tears blurred her vision. She struggled to get words past the lump in her throat but failed.

"I'm falling in love with you, Avery." Weston cupped her face in his hands. He swiped at her cheeks, wiping away the water on them. "My timing is terrible—"

"No," she choked out. Avery understood why he'd said it now. As law enforcement, they were intimately familiar with the knowledge that tomorrow isn't promised. She placed a hand over his heart, the fabric of Weston's shirt soft under her palm. "I did some soul-searching and praying myself last night. I'm falling in love with you too."

His breath hitched. "Avery—"

"I've been trying to figure out all morning if I should tell you." Her chin trembled. "I knew you were hurting and I didn't want to make it worse."

"You're always thinking about everyone else, sweetheart." His tone a mixture of affection and exacerbation. Weston wiped more tears from her cheeks. "When this is over, I'm going to take you out for a date. Our first date."

She laughed through her tears. "Chasing serial killers doesn't count, huh?"

"No, it doesn't. There's a candlelight

dinner with your name on it." He smiled, his thumb gently tracing her lower lip. "And the next present I buy you won't be a weapon."

He lowered his head and kissed her. Avery's legs went weak as her heart swelled with emotion. He undid her. Here, with Weston, she was safe and protected. There was a job to do, but for this one second, she allowed herself to forget about everything but him.

A knock on the door made them both jump. They called out "hold on" simultaneously and then grinned. Avery wrapped her arms around Weston's neck and pulled him down for another kiss. Her mouth brushed against his, and then she backed away.

She ran a hand over her hair and then her face. "Can you tell I've been crying? Or kissing you?"

"No." A smile curved his lips. "You look beautiful."

Their gazes caught and held. Her already accelerated heartbeat quickened. Avery opened her mouth, but Weston's cell phone rang, cutting her off. He glanced at the caller ID before his gaze shot to her. "It's your grandmother."

Avery stiffened. Nana wouldn't call Weston unless there was an emergency. He put the call on speaker. "Marla, what is it?"

"It's Savannah. We can't find her."

Weston drove to the church in five minutes flat, lights flashing and sirens blaring. The warmth of those stolen moments in the office with Avery were replaced by hard reality. He hadn't known Savannah very long but considered her a friend. Yet whatever worry he was feeling was a drop in the bucket compared to Avery.

"We'll get her back." Weston didn't take his eyes off the road. He couldn't at nearly sixty miles an hour in town.

"She's the knight." Avery's voice was hollow. "Knights were soldiers in medieval times. Savannah did three tours in a war zone only to come home and be kidnapped from her own church by a lunatic."

They didn't have confirmation Savannah had been taken by the Chessmaster, but in his heart, Weston knew she had. Troopers had been assigned to watch over Marla and Savannah until Rachel's disappearance. Finding the missing woman had taken priority, and every available law enforcement officer was pulled to pursue leads. It'd left Savannah vulnerable. Something Weston was mentally berating himself for.

He whipped into the church parking lot. Sheriff deputies held back reporters and townsfolk. Debra's funeral service had been cancelled. The church was a crime scene.

Weston circled to the rear of the church and stopped at the service entrance. Luke and Emilia were in the vehicle behind him.

Calvin met them at the door. The retired FBI agent went straight into a report. "We were setting up the reception area. The pastor's daughter asked Savannah to assist her in the kitchen with final food preparations. They left, but the pastor's daughter got sidetracked by another issue. Savannah went into the kitchen by herself. We discovered she was missing thirty minutes later."

"Did you conduct a search of the building?" Avery asked.

"There's no need." Calvin pointed to a camera overhead. "We have video. Come on."

He led them to the church office. Marla rose from the couch, tears staining her cheeks. "I'm so sorry, Avery. She was only gone—"

"No." Avery hugged her grandmother. "This isn't your fault."

"It's mine," Calvin said. "I shouldn't have let Savannah out of my sight."

"No one is to blame except the man who took her," Avery said. She passed a knowing glance at Weston. "No one."

Her words didn't relieve his guilt, but they put a dent in it. Weston pointed to the television on the wall. Four camera angles were frozen on screen. Two showed the church kitchen, two others were on the rear parking lot. "Time is of the essence. Let's see the video."

"I've got it cued up for you." Calvin hit a button on the computer.

On screen, Savannah appeared in the kitchen. She removed some trays from a high shelf and set them on the stainless-steel countertop. Out of camera range, something caught her eye. Her mouth moved. Weston surmised she was talking to someone. Beside him, Avery squinted, as if trying to read her sister's lips.

A man came into view wearing a blue hat, jeans, and a button-down. He was heavy-set and a beard covered the lower half of his face. Weston stepped closer to the screen. He'd seen the man before but couldn't place where.

Avery gasped. "It's Tom Belvin."

Luke shot her a glance. "Are you sure?"

"Positive. He's altered his appearance with a fat suit and beard, but it's definitely him." She pointed to the screen. "It's the way he walks. Like a bodybuilder."

"She's right," Weston said. "I couldn't place it, but I recognized him too."

On screen, Savannah nodded and turned her back. It was all the opportunity Tom needed. He grabbed her head and shoved it into the countertop. Savannah fought back and nearly escaped, but Tom jabbed her with a syringe. She went limp.

He carried Savannah out to the parking lot and loaded her into his SUV. The plates were spattered with mud. The entire incident, according to the clock on the security camera, lasted for two minutes.

Weston's fingers twitched, and he had the urge to ball his hands into fists. Instead, he turned to Calvin. "We need a still shot of Tom to hand out to all law enforcement, along with one of his vehicle."

"The pastor is already making copies in his office. I'll get them."

"I'll join you, Calvin." Luke turned to Marla. "Ma'am, can you come with us? I'd like to ask some follow-up questions."

"Of course." Marla swiped tears from her cheeks. "That man in the blue hat was here all morning helping to set up for the funeral. He seemed so nice."

They left the room, and Avery sank into a chair. "Well, that explains why Savannah let him get close to her. She had no reason to be on guard."

"It's not uncommon for killers to attend the funerals of their victims." Emilia stepped over to the computer. "Or in this case, assist in setting up one. It allows the killer to relive the murder."

She replayed the video. "He's deviated from his pattern, but it's still there. A blitz-style attack, using a rear door, and kidnapping the victim. And yet...something is bothering me." Emilia leaned against the table, her eyes glued to the screen. "I can't put my finger on it."

"Tom used his own SUV this time." Weston watched again as the attacker loaded Savannah into his vehicle. "The other times he used a delivery van with stolen plates."

"That's because a delivery van would've stuck out." Emilia pointed to the other vehicles in the lot. "Every other car is personal. He wanted to blend in."

"Everything about him is designed to blend in," Avery said. "The clothes. The beard hides the bottom half of his face. And the bodysuit he's wearing makes him appear out of shape and harmless."

Emalia nodded. "The disguise is to hide his identity, but the choice he made when selecting it supports your assertion, Avery. When did your sister and Nana decide to assist with the funeral?"

"They're part of the decoration committee for the church. It's standard for them to be here for a funeral."

"The problem is Tom doesn't fit the profile." Emilia squinted at the television screen. "He's mild-mannered. Other than the drug arrest, he has no criminal history. He's never physically abused any of his girlfriends. His boss described him as awkward and not prone to independent thinking. Tom's a follower, not a leader."

"So what are you saying?" Weston rocked back on his heels. "We have the wrong man?"

"No." Emilia frowned. "Profiling isn't an exact science, but personalities are important—"

Avery's cell phone rang. Weston's gaze shot to her as she pulled it out of her pocket. The caller's ID had been blocked. She answered, hitting the speaker option. "I'm going to lock you in a jail cell and watch you rot."

The Chessmaster laughed. With the voice distorter, it sounded mechanical and cold. "You have to catch me first. Your sister is my insurance policy. Theater building. Five minutes. No cops."

"I—"

"Do as I say or I'll kill both Savannah and Rachel. Ditch the ranger, Avery. You have five minutes."

NINETEEN

It took four minutes to get back to the university. Weston and Avery spent it coordinating
with Grady via cell phone. They needed to
trick Tom into believing they were following
his instructions. Undercover officers, dressed as
students and faculty, were being mobilized.

"Priority number one is keeping civilians
safe," Avery said. "There's no telling what Tom
has planned, and I won't put innocent lives at
risk. The second is capturing Tom alive. The
third is me."

She didn't want any confusion about what

the goals of this operation were. Police officers, no matter their uniform, were a family. They would try to protect Avery, and Tom might get away in the process.

"Understood," Grady said. "I'll make sure they know. Avery, there isn't time to wire you with a camera and microphone."

"I know. Tom designed it this way."

Noise came over the truck's speaker. It sounded like Grady was walking. "Weston, a change of clothes will be waiting for you in the music building. First floor, men's bathroom. An earpiece as well, so you can hear what's going on."

Avery couldn't imagine where Grady located an additional pair of clothes to fit Weston so quickly. She prayed the disguise would fool Tom into believing she'd ditched Weston as ordered.

Weston turned into a faculty parking lot. "Avery will be in the theater building on time. Thanks, Grady. Stay safe."

"You too."

Avery undid her seat belt with a snap and reached for the door handle, but Weston gently grabbed her elbow, halting her exit from the truck. The look in his eyes crushed her. Worry mixed with love.

"I'm counting on you to come out of this in one piece, Avery. Do you hear me?"

She kissed him, quick and hard. "Yes. Rumor has it, there's a candlelight dinner in my future." Avery took his hands in hers. "Can you lead us in prayer?"

Weston bowed his head. "Lord, wrap us in Your strength and wisdom. Help us do Your bidding. Protect those that are innocent, especially Rachel and Savannah. In Your name, we pray."

"Amen," Avery said. She took a deep breath. The heavy weight of responsibility bearing down on her shoulders wasn't gone, but it did feel lighter. "Let's do this."

She exited the truck and ran down the walkway. Weston veered off, headed to the music building. Avery slowed to an easy walk as she approached the theater building. Five minutes on the dot. Her hands were clammy, and she shook them out before tamping down on her jitters. There wasn't any room for self-doubt. The Chessmaster would use it against her.

Shoulders back and spine straight, Avery pulled open the door and stepped inside. Music and a cacophony of people greeted her, far more than expected on a Saturday afternoon. The scent of pizza drifted in the air. Where had all these people come from?

A corkboard hung on the wall and she scanned it. A flyer caught her attention. Open House Party. Free food. It wasn't one of the scheduled events.

Her phone rang and Avery glanced at the caller ID. Blocked.

She answered it. "You arranged for a crowd."

"I thought it'd be better that way."

It was. Easier for the Chessmaster to get lost during his escape. Her gaze swept the lobby. "And I was so hoping it would be just you and me."

"Soon it will be."

A shiver raced down her spine. The voice distorter only made his words creepier. She scanned the lobby again. There were so many people, it was hard to keep track.

There. A flash of blue on the second-floor landing caught her eye. The man was standing perfectly still in a sea of moving people. His back was to her, and a blue hat covered his hair, but Avery recognized him. He was still wearing the same shirt and jeans from earlier. Tom Belvin.

She stepped toward him, but a crowd of rowdy college men got in her way. She lifted her gaze back to the landing, but Tom was gone. Had any of the undercovers seen him?

"Go down the hall on your left," he ordered. "Quickly."

She followed his instructions, keeping to the center of the hallway. Victor's attack from a few days ago—was it only a few days?—was fresh in her mind. "Where is Rachel?"

"You'll see her soon. Go out the door at the end of the hallway, down the walkway, and into the athletic center."

Her footsteps faltered. The athletic center was under construction. It was closed off from the public. No one would be able to follow her inside. "I—"

"Now, Avery."

A click punctuated the order. He'd hung up. Avery gritted her teeth and shoved her cell phone back inside her pocket. There was no choice. Two innocent women were counting on her. She undid the snap on her gun holster, and jogged down the hall to the door.

The fire alarm in the theater building went off. Screams echoed from the lobby. Avery paused with her hand on the handle, but only for a second. Tom had made this move before at his house. The alarm would create chaos and draw law enforcement to the theater building.

Avery traversed the short distance to the

athletic center. A flock of crows lifted off from a nearby building, flying overhead like a bad omen. It sent a shiver down her spine. She typed a code into the panel on the door, and the lock released. The metal handle was cool against her heated palm.

Avery pulled her gun and, heart pounding, stepped inside.

The door shut behind her with a click. It echoed across the empty lobby, bouncing off the marble floor. She forced a deep breath. Was that...music?

It was faint but there. Hair rose on the back of Avery's neck as she moved through the lobby. The sensation of being watched plagued her. Her heart skittered as the location of the music became clear.

The pool.

Avery quickened her steps, racing to the pool area. The scent of chlorine burned her nose and humid air smacked her in the face. She stole a few precious seconds to clear the immediate area. Several closed doors led to locker rooms and other areas of the athletic center. She didn't have time to search thoroughly. There was something at the bottom of the pool.

She raced around the edge to the deep end. No, not something. Someone.

Rachel.

With shaking hands, Avery undid her service belt and boots. She set them on the edge, along with her gun and cell phone, and dove in. The water was murky from sitting stagnant during the building repairs.

Please, Lord. Please don't let me be too late.

She kicked, dragging herself down to the bottom. Her movements were slowed by the heavy weight of her uniform. Rachel was floating underwater, her eyes closed, hair swirling around her head. Avery's lungs burned for air. She'd never been a good swimmer.

She dove deeper, grabbing onto Rachel's feet. The woman was attached to some kind of weight. Avery used her fingers to trace the band around Rachel's ankle. Velcro. She squeezed her mouth shut and willed her body to hold on, despite the searing desire for air. Avery tugged on the band. The first one came off.

She moved to the second one, but her fingers couldn't find the edge. Desperation narrowed her vision. Avery's lungs were screaming. She closed her eyes and put her attention on the band. Her fingers tripped over the edge. She tore at it.

Rachel floated free. Avery grabbed the other woman and kicked for the surface. Panic clawed at her throat. She wasn't going to make it. Her clothes weighed her down, every move only seemed weaker.

At the last second, her head broke the water's edge. Avery dragged in a ragged breath. Then another. She was shaking. "Rachel? Rachel, can you hear me?"

The other woman was cold and still. Avery turned on her back, and put Rachel's head on her chest. With trembling fingers, she tried to check for a pulse but couldn't manage. Better to try again out of the water. She kicked across the pool to the stairs, sapped of strength. Still, she kept moving.

She needed to call for help. It wasn't until she was in the shallow end, Avery realized her cell was on the other side. Along with her gun.

She dragged Rachel out of the water and onto the tile. The woman wasn't breathing. Her lips were blue.

"No, you don't, Rachel. You stay with me."

Avery scrambled to clear Rachel's airway. She started doing CPR. Her focus was on one thing: saving Rachel's life. She completed one round of chest compressions. Then another. Her own heart thundered, her breathing raspy. "Please, Rachel. Come on!"

She bent down and breathed twice more in the woman's mouth. Rachel jerked. Avery turned her as Rachel threw up a mountain of pool water.

Tears ran down Avery's face. "Thank you, Lord. Thank you."

A noise came from behind her. Avery whirled as something slammed into the side of her head. Stars exploded across her vision. She toppled sideways, skating across the wet tile floor. Footsteps came closer. Avery kicked, but the move was weak and off-balance.

Her attacker straddled her. Something jabbed her neck. "Checkmate."

No. The jab had been from a syringe. He'd drugged her. *Rachel.*

Avery threw out an elbow and had the sweet satisfaction of hearing her attacker grunt. The success was short-lived. She scrambled to find purchase on the tile floor. Adrenaline sped the drug through her system. She swung with her fist, but it landed on his shoulder. Dark spots danced in front of her eyes.

"I don't have time for this," he growled.

The attacker grabbed her hair, throwing her head against the floor.

Everything went black.

Twenty minutes. That's how much time had passed since the last undercover officer had seen Avery. Weston clamped down on the dread clawing at his insides and focused on the task at hand. "Now that the firefighters have verified there's no fire, we need to do a room-by-room check, starting with the lobby and branching out."

Grady entered through the main doors. Weston pointed to him. "Coordinate with Ranger West to get it done."

The leader of the team nodded. "On it."

Weston watched as he moved toward the group of officers standing in the corner. The theater building felt huge, now that it was mostly devoid of people. He turned his attention back to the undercover. "Show me exactly where you saw Chief Madison last, Hank."

The undercover tugged on his T-shirt and marched across the marble floor. "She was right here." Hank pointed to the landing on the second floor. "It appeared something up there caught her notice. The chief moved in that direction but was cut off by a crowd of guys."

"And then?"

"She disappeared. One minute she was here, the next she wasn't. Then the fire alarm went off and everyone panicked."

Weston had entered the building, dressed in his undercover clothes, in time to witness the stampede. Frantic minutes were spent getting everyone out. It was a miracle no one had been seriously hurt.

Except for Avery.

No. He wouldn't go down that road. Weston needed to keep his attention on finding her. "Anything else you can think of, Hank? Anything that might help?"

"No, sir." He cleared his throat. "I'm sorry, sir."

Weston's heart was breaking, but he recognized the self-recrimination in the other man's voice. He clapped Hank on the shoulder. "You did your job, Officer. This isn't your fault. Chief Madison—"

His voice broke off, and Weston swallowed past the lump in his throat. "Chief Madison understood and accepted the risks of this operation. Now, join the rest of your team, and let's make sure she's not in the building somewhere."

"Yes, sir."

Weston glanced at the second-floor landing. He jogged up the stairs and circled to the point Hank had indicated.

He could see the entire lobby from here, including the door Avery would've used to enter. Had she spotted Tom? Or had something else gotten her attention? Weston scanned the immediate area, but there wasn't anything other than discarded pizza slices and soft drink cans.

Luke joined him. "The parking garage attached to the building is clear. No sign of Tom's SUV or a white van."

"That doesn't mean they weren't there."

"No." Luke blew out a breath. "It only takes fifteen minutes to drive from the church to the university. Tom would've had plenty of time to park in the garage and set things up to grab Avery. In the hysteria caused by the fire alarm, he could've slipped out with her. We're interviewing witnesses, but no one spotted a man lugging something or pushing a cart of any kind."

Weston frowned. How had Tom managed to get Avery out of the building? She wouldn't have gone quietly. And carrying a police officer out would've attracted some attention, even in the rush of a fire. He leaned against the railing.

Luke's brow wrinkled. "What are you thinking?"

"I'm not sure."

Weston went around his friend and jogged back down the stairs. The tennis shoes he was wearing as part of his undercover outfit made the job easier. Luke followed.

"This is where Hank last saw Avery. He said she was here one minute, gone the next." Weston turned in a circle. A hallway shot off to the left. He pointed to it. "Maybe that's why."

They ran down the corridor, clearing each room as they passed. No Avery. At the end was a door, sunlight streaming through the glass. Weston glanced out. Another building was a short distance away.

His heart jumped. "Luke, this way."

Weston raced across the walkway to the next building. It was locked, and signs hung on the doors announcing it was closed for repairs. He circled around the side and spotted cars. "Tom may have led Avery here. There's another parking lot in the back."

Luke grabbed his cell. "I'll get the code to unlock the door."

Weston paced outside the door, his stomach aching. He'd promised Avery a candlelight dinner. They were falling in love. Those few precious moments couldn't be all they would have.

Please, Lord. Keep Avery safe. I don't want to lose her.

Luke ran over to the panel and typed in a code. The door clicked open, and Weston grabbed it. He raced through the lobby yelling Avery's name.

She didn't answer. Music came from the rear of the building. Weston followed the sound, and a pool appeared. Someone was lying on the tile, long dark hair spread around her head.

Rachel Long.

Weston dropped to his knees beside her, and water saturated his pants. Rachel was soaking wet and unconscious, but breathing. "Luke, call EMS."

The woman was dressed in a long white gown. Weston shrugged off his jacket and placed it over her, his gaze already surveying the rest of the area. A pile of discarded objects caught his attention. His hands started shaking.

Weston rose and, on hollow legs, crossed to the other side of the pool. The gun, duty belt, and cell phone were immediately familiar.

They were Avery's.

TWENTY

Weston stood in the corner of the emergency room waiting area. A television played softly, and several individuals were clustered on the plastic chairs. One looked to have a broken hand, another was nursing the flu.

An ambulance drove up. EMTs raced past with a gurney. Weston was half-tempted to join the group, muscle his way back with a flash of his badge and talk to Rachel.

But she was unconscious. Or at least, she had been when they'd arrived two hours ago.

Weston blew out a breath and raked a hand

through his hair. He turned toward the window, lifting his gaze to the sky and said another prayer. He tamped down the voice inside his head reminding him that prayers hadn't saved Melissa. Those thoughts wouldn't get him anywhere except broken. His faith was the only thing keeping him on his feet.

Weston's phone rang and he answered it. "Donovan."

"We've located Tom's SUV," Grady said, skipping any pleasantries. "It was tucked between two dumpsters at the university. No sign of Savannah but Tom was in the rear. Strangled to death."

Weston closed his eyes. He pitched his voice low enough no one else in the emergency room could hear him. "So Emilia was right. Tom wasn't the Chessmaster. He was working with someone."

"Appears that way. There's more. The entire SUV was wiped clean, but the killer missed a spot. Under the passenger side seat. We got a good print. It belongs to Mike Steel."

Weston's mind raced. "That's an unlikely partnership."

"Not necessarily. They both had an ax to grind with Avery." Grady's tone was clipped. "Mike was angry he'd lost the Chief of Police position to her. Tom blamed Avery for his father's death. And the two men know each other."

"Mike arrested Tom and Nolan when they were kids."

"Exactly. We suspected the Chessmaster was someone on the inside with a working knowledge of police procedure. Mike fits Emilia's profile. Smart, college educated, etc. My guess is Mike developed the plan and Tom assisted him."

"Mike convinced Tom to kidnap Savannah, wearing a disguise." Weston could see the images of the attack against Avery's sister play out in his mind. "Tom drives to the university and switches Savannah from his SUV to the white van. Then he acts as a lookout for Mike in the theater building."

"Sounds right. It explains how the killer was able to move so fast."

Weston's hand tightened on the phone. "It also explains why Avery had time to pull Rachel out of the pool. Killing Tom delayed Mike."

"We've got roadblocks set up on the freeway and around town. We're stopping every white delivery van."

Too late. Mike had everything he needed. "We should check every unoccupied house on Tom's mail route. If Mike is the Chessmaster, he needs a place to..."

Kill. The word wouldn't move past his throat.

"I'm already on it," Grady said.

Weston stared out the window. A couple was making their way across the parking lot. Partners. He mulled it over, but something didn't quite fit. "Can we link Mike and Tom together? Other than the fingerprint in Tom's car and the arrest from twenty years ago?"

"Not yet, but Luke used the print to get a

search warrant for Mike's house. He's headed there now. I'm sending a photo array to your phone. Show it to Rachel. Hopefully, she can identify Mike as her attacker."

A doctor called out Weston's name. He said a quick goodbye to Grady as he crossed the waiting room. "That's me."

"It's my understanding you wanted to speak to Mrs. Long. Please come with me."

The man turned on his heel. Weston hurried to catch up to the doctor's long strides. "How is she?"

"Hard to say. Medically, she's stable." He paused outside an exam room. "Mrs. Long awoke and was initially responsive but then suffered a panic attack. She struck one of the nurses and was screaming and crying uncontrollably. We had to sedate her."

"Any idea what triggered the panic attack?"

The doctor shrugged. "She's been through a serious trauma. Sometimes the effects can be delayed."

Weston nodded and stepped inside the

room. Rachel's petite form was barely a lump on the bed. Her dark hair was spread across the pillow. Various tubes drifted out from under the blankets and a heart monitor beat in a steady rhythm.

"Mrs. Long, my name is Texas Ranger Weston Donovan. There are some questions I need to ask you."

The woman didn't move. He went around the bed and stood directly in front of her. Rachel's eyes were glassy. Weston bit back his frustration and kept his tone calm but authoritative.

"Ma'am, I'm sorry, but it's very important. The man who hurt you has kidnapped two other women." Weston took a risk and stepped closer to the bed. He didn't want to crowd Rachel, but he needed her to understand the urgency of the situation. "One of them is your friend, Savannah Madison. The other is Chief of Harrison University Police Avery Madison. Avery pulled you out of the pool tonight. She saved your life."

Rachel's eyes flickered down and then settled on him. Progress. He would take it. "Where were you being held?"

No response.

"Was it a house?"

Nothing. Rachel lifted her hand and grabbed his. She squeezed, her nails digging into his skin. Desperation oozed out of her. Rachel wanted to tell him something, Weston could sense that much. But fear, or perhaps the medication they'd given her, was making communication difficult.

"Let's try this," Weston said softly. "Squeeze my hand once for yes and twice for no. Can you do that?"

One squeeze. His heart leaped, but Weston kept his expression and tone soothing. "That's good, Rachel. That's very good. Were you held in a house?"

One squeeze.

"Was it in a neighborhood?"

Nothing. Maybe she didn't know.

"Can you identify the man who attacked you?"

One squeeze.

Weston pulled out his phone. He brought up the photo array Grady had sent him and showed it to Rachel. Mike was in the center, number three. Weston slipped his hand back into hers. "Is the man who attacked you in one of these pictures?"

Her gaze flickered to the phone and her forehead creased. Two squeezes. Weston froze. "Are you sure?"

Two squeezes, this time more forcefully. He stared at her. "Can you tell me your attacker's name?"

The door to the room swung open and a nurse entered. She stopped short. "Oh, I'm sorry to interrupt. I need to take vitals." She moved closer to the bed. "How are you, Mrs. Long? Feeling better?"

Rachel didn't answer. Weston frowned. "The doctor mentioned Rachel had a panic attack earlier."

"Yes, sir." The nurse wrapped a cuff around Rachel's arm. "A patient in the emergency room started watching the news on their phone. Mrs. Long overheard and she became very upset."

Weston glanced at Rachel again. Her dark eyes were focused on him, fear lurking in their depths. Then they flickered to the television and her hand trembled in his. Could she have seen a news story about her own disappearance? Or was it more than that?

The nurse finished her exam, and the door clicked closed behind her.

Weston took a deep breath. He didn't want to scare the young woman. She'd been traumatized enough, but he needed her help. Lives depended on it. "Was your attacker on television, Rachel?"

One squeeze.

He picked up the remote. "May I turn on the news so we can watch it together?"

She didn't move, then a squeeze. Lighter than all the others. Weston let out the breath he was holding. "Thank you, Rachel. Whoever he is, I promise you, he cannot hurt you ever again. I'll make sure of it."

He clicked on the television. Breaking news was playing about the fire alarm at the university. The newscaster filled in the details. No response from Rachel.

The story changed to the missing women and the murders. The newscaster droned on. "Our correspondent, Greg Kilbourne, completed an interview yesterday with Harrison University Police Chief, Avery Madison. Here's some of what he learned."

The shot changed to one of Greg standing outside the university. He kept his expression appropriately somber, but even through the screen, Weston sensed the reporter's thrill at nailing the interview. A little tag on the right corner labeled it previously recorded.

Rachel squeezed his hand.

Weston's gaze shot to her. Tears were leaking from her eyes, dripping onto the pillow. She couldn't even look at the television.

"Rachel, is your attacker Greg Kilbourne?"

One squeeze.

Awareness came like moving through a soupy fog. Every muscle in Avery's body ached, and her head felt like someone was beating it with a hammer. She groaned.

"Wakey, wakey."

A pair of hands shook her shoulders, and her head flopped back and forth. She struggled to right it. The clatter of metal against metal only increased her confusion. Where was she? Her thoughts were scattered like confetti on the wind, too difficult to chase. All she wanted to do was sleep and escape the pain. That wasn't too much to ask.

Someone lightly smacked her cheek. Avery forced her eyes open. The fierce pounding inside her skull increased, and she winced, as light assaulted her. She blinked. Then again. A man's face loomed in front of her, and Avery reared back. She tried to move her hands but couldn't.

Tied. She was tied.

It came back to her in a horrifying kaleidoscope of memories. Pulling Rachel from the pool, being attacked, and then drugged. Her breathing increased. Avery blinked again, willing her eyes to adjust to the light and her head to stop pounding. The man standing in front of her came into focus.

Greg Kilbourne.

"Well, hello, Avery." Greg's tone was mocking. "Nice of you to join us."

She tried to speak, but her tongue was fuzzy and slow. A side effect of the drug. Her body shook uncontrollably. From fear or cold, she couldn't tell. Her clothes were still damp from the pool. She struggled to piece together the puzzle. Why would Greg Kilbourne try to kill her? Where was Tom?

Greg laughed, then grabbed a lock of Avery's hair. He gave it a gentle tug. "Poor thing. You're confused. Allow me to enlighten you."

Greg removed his glasses and threw them to the side. They clattered against the floor. Then he reached up and tugged at his beard. He peeled it from his face, revealed a long scar across his chin.

Her heart rate skyrocketed. "N-N-N-Nolan."

Jack Starin's son. Nolan closed his eyes and a smile crept across his face. "Ahhh, I've waited a long time for you to say my real name."

Not all of his features were the same. His nose was different and his cheeks were chubbier. The plastic surgery—coupled with the beard, glasses, and green contact lenses—had been an effective disguise.

She blinked again. Nolan Starin was alive.

He smirked in acknowledgment of her unvoiced thought. "Yes, I faked my own death. One of the many things I learned to do while in prison."

Avery took deep breaths to counteract the drug swimming in her system. She wet her cracked lips with her tongue. "W-Where's my sister?"

"Oh, she's right here. Along with a surprise guest, I'm sure you'll be happy to see."

Nolan backed away, enabling Avery to view the room. It was small with two doors on the right-hand side. The only window had been boarded up, and the floor was tile.

Savannah sat against the far wall. A bruise bloomed along the side of her face and dried blood clumped her hair together. Silver tape covered her mouth, and she was shackled. Twist ties looped around her wrists and feet. A chain was threaded through them and encircled her waist. It was secured to an eyehook in the center of the floor with a padlock. Savannah shifted her hands and the chain rattled. Her wrists were bloody.

Avery met her sister's gaze. Savannah was trying to hide it, but she was terrified. Avery shared the feeling but wouldn't allow it to take root. She couldn't. Her sister was alive, and although the situation appeared impossible, it wasn't over. Not yet.

Sitting beside Savannah was Mike Steel. He was unconscious and also bound. Tape covered his mouth.

Avery's gaze shot to Nolan. He chuckled. "You see, I captured your knight." He pointed to Savannah, then shifted his finger to Mike. "And your queen. It's unorthodox, I'll admit, picking Mike to be that piece. But he was your father's partner. And you worked with him as well from time to time."

Nolan was going to kill them. Avery glanced down at her own restraints. Unlike her sister and Mike, she was sitting in a chair. Her feet were attached to the legs with twist ties. She strained her fingers and discovered more ties around her wrists securing them to the chair.

"You cap—" Avery shook her head and then winced. It felt as though someone had used her skull as a bowling ball. She took another deep breath and forced her tongue to work. "You captured Mike after we met with him at his house?"

That's why the lawyer wouldn't allow them to question him. He hadn't been able to locate his client.

Nolan smiled. "It was fun watching you and the rangers spin your wheels to find him."

"You won't get away with this. Every police officer in three counties is looking for us."

"Like they were looking for Debra and Marianne." He scoffed. "I'm not worried. My alter ego isn't even on the suspect list."

He was right. Greg Kilbourne had never been a suspect. How would the rangers find them? Weston must be out of his mind with worry. Tears pricked Avery's eyes, but she forced them back. Now was not the time to think about Weston and the kisses they shared, the promises they'd made—

She stiffened. Weston.

Please, Lord, please...

Avery leaned back against the chair. The knife Weston had given her pressed into her skin. She wanted to weep with relief. Instead, she kept her gaze on Nolan. "You've worked hard to kidnap us."

"I did." He kicked Mike in the stomach. The detective groaned, and Nolan kicked him again. "Stop faking. I know you're awake."

Mike opened his eyes and swung with his fists. Nolan scooted out of the way and laughed. Avery took advantage of the distraction. Her fingers fumbled with the edge of her shirt. The twist ties cut into her skin.

No! The angle was wrong. She couldn't reach the knife.

"Let them go, Nolan." Avery adjusted her position on the chair. "This is between you and me."

He pinned her with a look. "Haven't you figured it out yet? Avery, Avery, Avery. I thought you would be a worthy opponent. Now, I'm starting to think you're as stupid as the rest."

Nolan circled closer and his gaze narrowed. Avery froze. The knife was her only chance. If he discovered it, there would be no stopping him.

She forced herself to meet his gaze. "You're angry about your dad's death."

"My dad's *murder*." His hands balled into fists. "Your father shot him in cold blood."

Not true. Her father had killed Jack Starin in self-defense. But arguing that point would be frivolous. Nolan was beyond logic.

"I was just a kid when your dad died," Avery said. "I didn't have anything to do with it."

"Blood vengeance. Isn't that what they call it?" She flinched as Nolan grabbed the badge pinned to her shirt. He ripped it off. "You and me. We're stand-ins for our fathers. I continued my dad's work. You continued yours."

"You kill innocent women while I work to put monsters like you away."

He threw her badge to the ground. "Something like that." Nolan leaned down until they were face-to-face. The look in his eyes iced Avery's blood. "I will destroy your spirit, and then I'll take your life."

He placed a hand around Avery's throat. Her heartbeat thrummed against his fingers, and although she tried to hide her fear, she knew Nolan could sense it. He squeezed her throat.

"Soon," he whispered. "Soon, I'll watch the last breath leave your body. But first, the game we've been playing isn't over yet." He released her, his lips forming a cruel smile. "I'm going to kill Mike and Savannah. And, Avery, you're going to watch."

TWENTY-ONE

Avery's insides quaked as bile rose in her throat. What Nolan described was her own personal nightmare. She couldn't watch him kill her sister and Mike.

She wouldn't.

Lord, help me find a way out of this.

Nolan whistled as he crossed the room and touched a button on the wall. A noose, attached to a pulley system on the ceiling, lowered. Dread washed through Avery. Mike glared from his corner of the room, hatred oozing out of every pore.

Avery needed to delay Nolan long enough to get the knife, or until help arrived. She racked her brain, thinking about everything she knew about Nolan. He and his father had strategized crimes together. They'd been arrogant and believed themselves better than everyone else.

People were capable of change. Nolan had gotten much better at killing and hiding his crimes, but deep down, she bet he was still the same. Cocky and prone to flashes of anger.

Avery shifted lower in her chair. "Was Mike in on your plan?"

The detective's glare shifted to Avery, but she ignored him, keeping her focus on Nolan. She already knew Mike wasn't involved, but she needed a distraction.

Nolan arched his brows. "Are you stalling for time? Help's not coming, Avery."

"I know, but color me curious. We've been opponents this entire time, and you've played the game beautifully." She shrugged. "Figured you would want to share the details of each move. So, was Mike in on your plan?"

Nolan was quiet for a long moment. Avery held her breath. *Come on. You know you want to tell me.*

Nolan cast Mike a dismissive glance. "No, Mike wasn't involved. Not exactly. He's angry because I befriended and used him."

Avery let out the breath she was holding. "How?"

"After I faked my death, I took a little vacation in Mexico. Had some work done." He ran a finger down his nose. "Got a fake ID, then moved to Union County. I'd studied law enforcement procedures while in prison, but I had questions."

Avery's gaze snagged on Savannah. The two women had always been close and shared an innate ability to read each other's minds. The terror in her sister's expression had shifted to purpose. Savannah jerked her chin toward the door closest to her.

The exit? Had to be.

Avery twisted her fingers under her shirt. "Mike could answer your questions."

"Told him I was writing a book. You'd be surprised what people will share with a reporter. Of course it helped that we played chess together sometimes."

Avery's gaze darted to the detective. "After we confronted Mike in his home, he suspected you knew something, but he wasn't sure. He came to question you."

"I was counting on it. You had enough information to make him wonder. But we were friends, so he didn't give you my name."

"Mike didn't want to drag you into the investigation if you were innocent."

"Foolish mistake there, Mike. You should never trust anyone." Nolan raised a hand and pulled on the noose, testing the resistance. He grinned at Avery. "When Mike arrived, I got the drop on him."

So much started to make sense and fall into place. "When you told me about the notes outside Rachel's house, I thought the information had come from Mike. But it hadn't. You knew their contents because you'd written them."

He laughed. "Yes, but I played the part of a local reporter well. Didn't I?"

Her fingers brushed against the hilt of the knife. Almost there. "Why now? I've been a cop for a long time."

"Well, I was in prison for a while. That took up some of my time." He smirked. "I also wasn't going to make the same mistake twice. I'd learned from my past, unlike my dad. Killing needs patience. Strategy. Planning. A lot like chess. When you moved back to town, I knew fate had presented me with the right opportunity."

Avery shifted a little lower in her chair. Her wrists were going numb from the awkward positioning, but she refused to give up. She flexed her fingers and stretched. "What about Tom? How does your half-brother fit into all of this?"

The ties cut deeper, and warm liquid dripped across her skin. Two of her fingers grasped the hilt. She shifted and the knife slid partly out of the sheath.

Careful, careful.

She took a deep breath. "Tom kidnapped Savannah, but I don't think he did it willingly. You ambushed him outside of the post office and terrorized him. The church had cameras. You couldn't risk taking Savannah yourself."

Nolan's expression darkened. "Tom was an embarrassment to the family. My father gave him chance after chance, but Tom was a weakling. I manipulated him into helping me, and then I got rid of him."

Nolan was demented. How many people would he kill? She had no illusions. This wasn't about vengeance, not really. It was the thrill he was after. Nolan had a taste for murder, and he'd keep going until he was in jail or dead.

Her fingers trembled, and Avery inched her way up in the chair. More of the knife came out of the sheath. "I saw Tom in the theater building. When did you have time to kill him?"

Nolan arched his brows. "While you were fishing Rachel out of the pool."

That explained how she was able to do CPR. But...had Nolan killed Rachel after attacking Avery? Her stomach clenched at the thought. "Aren't you worried Rachel will be able to identify you?"

He waved a hand dismissively. "She never saw my face. I wore a mask. Besides, that's a loose end I can clean up later."

Avery sent up a prayer of thanksgiving. Whatever else, Rachel was alive. Weston would keep her under protection.

"Enough chit chat." Nolan released the noose, and clapped his hands together. "Time for some fun. Now who wants to be first?"

Avery jerked upward in her chair. "Wait, you haven't told me everything. What about the phone calls? How did you manage to hide where they were coming from?"

She let desperation bleed into her voice. Nolan wanted her fear. Well, she would give it to him. Anything to buy more time. The knife wasn't free yet.

Nolan grinned. "Don't worry, Avery. After we kill one, we can talk some more."

He turned on his heel, and Mike lunged at him. Nolan sidestepped and grabbed the man in a choke hold. "Ah, a volunteer."

Avery's heart went into overdrive. Time was up. Sweat dripped down her back as she blocked out everything in the room and focused solely on getting the knife out of the sheath. She wiggled in the chair.

Almost. Almost.

She held her breath and slid left. The knife came free and she gripped it. She met Savannah's gaze briefly and then sliced through the ties on her wrist as Nolan slipped the noose over Mike's neck. He tightened it.

"Don't look away, Avery." Nolan hit the button on the wall. Mike's feet left the ground and he clawed at the rope. "You don't want to miss it."

Savannah flung herself at Nolan. Avery

used the distraction to cut through the bonds on her legs. Her movements were jerky and she slit her calf. It started bleeding. She ignored it, launching herself across the room, but her feet had gone numb.

She tripped. Nolan rushed her, and she slashed at him with the knife. It sank into his thigh. He screamed, his face turning red.

She ducked as he swung a fist. Keeping hold of the knife, she ripped it from his leg and shoved his body with her shoulder. He fell to the ground, cursing. Avery staggered to her feet and raced to the button on the wall. She slammed the heel of her hand into it.

Mike dropped to the ground. He came up on all fours, coughing.

Avery's vision swam. She was going to pass out. The knocks to her head, coupled with whatever drug Nolan had pumped her full of, was still affecting her. She blinked to clear her vision.

A muffled scream came from Savannah. Avery half-turned in time to see a flash of color as Nolan tackled her. Together they went sliding across the room. The knife flew out of her hand and skittered across the floor.

Nolan punched her in the face so hard her teeth knocked together. He wrapped his hands around her throat. "I'm going to kill you."

She bucked and struggled to free her own hands. They were trapped on either side of her body by Nolan's legs, and she was too weak to fight him off.

Avery grew lightheaded, dark spots growing across her vision. Her sister's muffled screams disappeared. She desperately shook her head and kicked her legs. Nolan smiled, and his grip tightened.

Air. She needed air.

A primal roar echoed in the room one heartbeat before Nolan was flung away. Avery dragged in a breath. Then another. A swirl of commotion surrounded her, but none of it made sense. Voices barking out orders, someone yelling. Darkness still clouded her vision. She couldn't do anything but focus on drawing oxygen into her lungs.

"Avery." The word was a whisper, almost a prayer. "Open your eyes. Look at me."

Weston. He touched her face, brushing hair off her cheek. It took effort, but Avery opened her eyes a slice. The edges of his face were blurry. He'd found her. He'd saved her.

I love you.

Tears dripped on her face. His tears.

"I need an EMT now! I think her windpipe's damaged." He cupped her face. "Keep breathing, Avery. Just keep breathing."

TWENTY-TWO

One month later

Sunshine streamed across the backyard. The scent of hamburgers drifted on the wind. There was a nip in the air, but not enough to dissuade anyone from enjoying the outdoors. Weston tucked the blanket around the baby nestled in his arms. Ava studied his face with wide eyes. "It's okay, sweet girl. I'm giant-sized, but I'm no ogre."

Luke shook his head. "Don't listen to him, Ava. He used to tackle people for a living."

"True, but my guess is, in about sixteen years, your daddy's gonna be grateful for my skills at knocking men out of the way."

The two rangers laughed. Ava fussed, and Luke held out his hands. "That's our cue to find Mama. I think Ava's hungry."

Weston passed the baby over and watched as Luke carried his daughter across the yard and into the house. Grady was stationed behind the grill, tongs in hand, wearing a ridiculous hot dog apron. His wife, Tara, said something that made him laugh. Troopers and sheriff's deputies filled paper plates with food. Neighbors chatted.

He spotted his boss, Lieutenant Rodriguez, and Emilia at a picnic table. Weston moved to join them.

"Uncle Weston, Uncle Weston."

The voice carried across the lawn. Weston braced himself as a ball of cyclone energy in pigtails tackled his leg. Grady's daughter,

Maddy, grinned up at him. "Avery and I colored a new drawing for you."

"Did you now?" He craned his neck. "Where is Avery?"

Avery appeared on the back porch. Her hair was loose around her shoulders, and when she caught sight of him, a smile lit up her face. It reached inside Weston and squeezed his heart tight. He loved her smile. Loved making her smile.

Avery brushed a kiss on Weston's cheek before turning to the little tyke still hanging on his leg. "Maddy, should I give him the picture?"

The little girl nodded. Avery flipped the paper around. A couple holding hands was standing in a field next to a house. Maddy pointed to the woman in the dress. "That's Avery." Her finger moved to the giant man standing next to her. "And that's you."

Avery winked. "Did you notice you're the same size as the house?"

He chuckled. "I see that. Thank you,

Maddy. It's wonderful. I'll hang it on my fridge at home."

The little girl scampered off to play with some of the other kids. Weston wrapped his arms around Avery. It centered his world to have her close. "How's your sister? Is she feeling better?"

Avery nodded. "She just needed to lie down. The pregnancy is making her a bit green around the gills."

Savannah had found out she was pregnant a few days before Nolan kidnapped her, but didn't share the news with anyone. Not even her husband. After walking out of Nolan's house, it was the first thing she said when Henry called. He was due to be home before the little one was born.

Avery tightened her hold on Weston's waist. "Rachel called a little while ago. She's back from vacation and asked if we could get together soon."

"I'd like that."

Rachel Long had become a good friend in

the last few weeks. She'd recognized Greg Kilbourne aka Nolan Starin as her captor from his voice alone. She told investigators later that when she heard him on the news, it triggered a panic attack.

Weston didn't like to think about those harrowing moments when he'd broken into the rear bedroom of Nolan's house. Seeing the killer on top of Avery, choking the life from her, was seared into his brain. He'd slammed into Nolan and set him flying so hard into the opposite wall, it'd left a hole in the sheetrock.

Avery had nearly died. Her windpipe had been severely damaged, but she'd made a full recovery. So had Savannah and Mike. Nolan was charged with multiple counts of murder, kidnapping, and other charges. He would be behind bars forever.

Weston pulled Avery closer, cupping her cheek. "What are the chances we can sneak away for a candlelight dinner later?"

Her eyes sparkled. "I think that can be arranged."

He ran a thumb over her bottom lip and bent his head to kiss her, but a voice called his name. Weston rested his forehead against Avery's. "Whose idea was it to invite all these people anyway?"

Avery chuckled. "I think it was yours. And Nana's." She slipped out of his arms but took his hand. "Come on. Nana wants to say a few words."

Weston swallowed hard and let Avery lead him across the yard. His heartbeat increased with every step. His boots thumped against the porch steps, and he tamped down the jittery nerves flapping in his stomach.

Avery's grandmother, Marla, clapped her hands together to get everyone's attention. "Okay, okay. Thank you all for coming. We wanted to celebrate today, because there is so much to be grateful for." Tears filled the older woman's eyes. "My two granddaughters are here with me, safe and sound, and all of you had a hand in making that happen. Thank you from the bottom of my heart."

The crowd clapped and cheered. Marla waved them into silence again.

"An especially big shout-out goes to this handsome ranger right here." She placed a hand on his arm. "Weston Donovan, I said it before, but this time, I'm making it public. As far as I'm concerned, you're an honorary member of the Madison family."

"Hear, hear," yelled Savannah.

Weston took a deep breath to calm his racing heart. "Thank you, ma'am. And while I appreciate being an honorary member of the Madison family, I was actually hoping to become more."

He turned to Avery and took both of her hands in his. Weston dropped to one knee. A collective gasp came from the crowd, and a sudden lump formed in his throat. He'd practiced these words a hundred times, but now that the moment was here, Weston wasn't sure he could say them.

How could he explain how she'd changed him? Describe the wealth of emotion that swept over him whenever he saw her? Words weren't good enough, but they were all he had. They would have to do.

Avery's hands shook and he squeezed them gently.

"Avery, from the moment we met, I knew you were someone special. I'd abandoned the idea of love or marriage or a family. Completely. Then you marched up my driveway armed with a murder case, and changed the course of my life."

There were a few chuckles. Weston kept his gaze locked on the woman in front of him. He had to get this right.

"You've blown me away with your kindness and your bravery. A good friend once told me, love is like faith. It's a choice. Well, I choose you. Every day. Every minute. For the rest of my life. And I'm hoping and praying you feel the same way."

Tears filled Avery's eyes and her chin trembled. He released her hands and reached into his pocket to pull out a black jewelry case. He opened it. The diamond nestled inside winked.

"Will you do me the honor of becoming my wife?"

Weston held his breath. His hands trembled slightly. There wasn't a sound from the crowd.

Avery met his gaze, blinking past her tears. "Yes. Yes, I'll marry you."

A collective cheer rose from their family and friends. Avery reached for Weston's wrists, tugging him to his feet. He kissed her, wrapping his arms around her. One hand still held the diamond ring, the other nestled in her hair. When he pulled back, they were both breathless.

"I love you, Avery."

She brushed her lips against his once more. "I love you too, Weston."

ALSO BY LYNN SHANNON

Available Now

Vanish

Ranger Protection

Ranger Redemption

Ranger Courage

Ranger Faith

Ranger Honor

Coming 2021

Ranger Loyalty

Would you like to know when my next book is released? Or when my novels go on sale? It's easy. Subscribe to my newsletter at www. lynnshannon.com and all of the info will come straight to your inbox!

Reviews help readers find books. Please consider leaving a review at your favorite place of purchase or anywhere you discover new books. Thank you.

CPSIA information can be obtained
at www.ICGtesting.com
Printed in the USA
LVHW031733030223
738606LV00002B/182